Before The Boy

Before The Boy

The Chilling Prequel to the Moon Singer Trilogy

B. Roman

Even in death a mother guides her son through triumphs and tragedies to his true destiny.

Prologue - Present Day

Billie Nickerson has three minutes to live. It won't be fast and it won't be painless to die. She knew this day would come, but not that it would be today or this way.

She has lived 100 lifetimes that she cannot remember and will live 100 more before she has paid her Karmic debts. But in moments, this life - her most pivotal incarnation, the one that makes every past life immaterial and every future life a stepping stone to eternity- will end.

Billie's daughter, Sally, who brings a sunshiny light into every room just by entering, sleeps peacefully in the back seat. Just a few days into her teen years now, she will be crippled, her legs mangled, an unintended consequence.

Sally's older brother, David, a music prodigy despite his deafness who is destined for a greatness that he cannot imagine at this moment, sits by her side, daydreaming about how he will execute a new music piece Billie has taught him. His life will be spared but he will hate his mother forever for dying.

Billie has just a few seconds left now to be with her cherished husband, Isaac, who deftly steers the car down the treacherous winding road home.

"Please buckle your seat belt, Billie," Isaac admonishes. "I don't know what I'll encounter in this fog."

"I will, Isaac. I just have to adjust it. It's too tight and I can't get it to expand far enough for comfort."

"Can't it wait until we stop? Just put the damn thing back in the buckle for now. It's not like you to be careless."

"It's not like you to be so adamant about driving in this fog for a bunch of papers." It's the last time Billie will chastise Isaac for being so wed to his job.

"They're not just papers. They're important blueprints for the ship design that could set us on the road to financial independence."

Isaac turns to look at Billie, not knowing it's the last time he will see her face unscarred, and fails to see the headlights in his rearview mirror. He slows down to find the freeway exit, but misses the turn.

The impact from behind is instant and powerful. The semi plows into the Nickerson car with such force it becomes an uncontrollable projectile. Isaac's air bag deploys and he is momentarily blinded then passes out from the shock of the crash. Billie is thrust forward almost through the windshield but is forced down between the dashboard and the front seat. The passenger side airbag fails to deploy, a convenient stroke of fate.

When Billie's pulmonary vein tears she feels the blood gushing through her chest with such force a huge wave of nausea overtakes her. In a suffocating blow her heart is thrust from left to right, rupturing blood vessels and threatening to dissect her aorta.

In an instinctive move, David reaches for his sister but is restrained by the lap and shoulder harness. He will feel the pain from a fractured sternum and neck lacerations later. But for now he is ensconced in a confused world of silence, seeing and feeling the carnage around him but unable to hear the blast of the semi's horn, the screeching of tires on the highway, the steel upon steel as the vehicles collide and tear the guardrails out of their foundations. Nor does he hear the sirens of the emergency responders as they arrive on the scene.

The semi hangs precariously over an embankment but the driver is pulled from the cab miraculously alive and alert. The Nickerson SUV has suffered the worst of the crash, and is almost unrecognizable as a car.

"Jesus. The engine is almost cut in two. Cut the damn horn," one paramedic shouts. " I can't hear myself think!"

The other paramedic pulls futilely on the crumpled doors, desperate to assess if there are any survivors. "We need another bus," he yells. "There are four of them."

With blood oozing from her nose and mouth, Billie groans and thrashes her arms around, jerking out the drip the paramedic tries to insert into her arm while she is still trapped in the vehicle. Her utterings are incomprehensible and incoherent.

"What is she saying?"

His partner, trying to calculate how to free her from the wreck, just shakes his head. "I can't understand her. She's in shock. I don't see any visible head injury, just a big gash on her cheek. Blood seeping from her nostrils. Guarantee you there are some badass internal injuries."

"Leave me alone!" Billie implores, willing to die. She knows this is her end and she accepts it as prophecy, as the only way to save her family and to allow David to receive the extraordinary intuitive gifts he was born to inherit.

"I've got to get her to accept some treatment." The paramedic injects drugs to reduce her agitation and places an oxygen mask over her face. "See what you can do for the others."

"Jaws of Life will need to pry them out. Here comes the crew."

Like scissors cutting paper, the sharp blades on the Jaws pop open the twisted back doors. David and Sally are pulled out and they are placed on gurneys. Isaac is removed from the mangled vehicle after being disentangled from the deployed air bag. With sirens blaring, the first ambulance transports the three of them to the hospital trauma unit as the emergency responders work feverishly on getting Billie removed without injuring her further.

Billie's heart stops for the first time as she is taken out of the wreck of the SUV. Immediate cardiac massage is applied and her heart restarted. Sirens blare and lights flash from the rig as the driver races against time, but Billie's condition deteriorates again. By the time she arrives at the ER, trauma staff are on hand ready for a worst-case scenario. Surgeons slice open her chest and work feverishly to repair the tears and ruptures. But the loss of blood is too great and they hold out little hope.

"She's going down!"

Don't fight it Billie. I am here with you. Just let go."

"Stop compressions…check pulse…" There is none.

That's it, dear. Just a few more seconds now and we can walk your path together.

"Charge paddles to 300…clear!" Repeated electric shocks fail to revive Billie and she flatlines. Reluctantly, the doctors accept they can do no more to save her life.

"Want to call it?"

"Time of death 17:40."

God. Am I really dead? I'm floating but my body is lying flat in the hospital bed. Everyone thinks I'm dead, but I'm not. I want to shout that I'm alive. Don't pull that sheet over my face.

"Wait, wait!" The pulse on the monitor is weak but measurable. One doctor checks her eye response while the other checks Billie's respiration.

"No response in the pupils. No brain activity."

" No breath sounds. Yet the monitor shows a pulse."

The doctor places his stethoscope on Billie's chest. "It's erratic and faint. It's not possible. But let's intubate and maybe…"

Don't hesitate, Billie. Your time on this Earth is done.

No. Wait. I'm afraid. I don't want to leave yet.

I know. But remember this is what you wanted. And it's my task to make your transition easy, to take you where you are meant to reside for eternity. Soon you will have no memory of the pain of Earth, your death, or your family's grief.

Isaac sits on an ER gurney just steps away from Billie's treatment room. Suffering only facial contusions and burns on his hands from the deployed air bag, he is devastated and guilt ridden. How could Billie's air bag not deploy? Was there a recall notice? Did I forget to have it checked? Isaac ruminates painfully over every memory leading up to the crash. "I've killer her," he sobs. "I've killed my wife!"

Immobile in her ICU bed, Sally is sedated to keep her spine as still as possible, but will awaken to find she is paralyzed from the waist down. Her spinal injury might not have been as severe had she been sitting upright in the back seat instead of sleeping in a fetal position. The impact threw her forward into the driver's seatback and stretched her seat belt to its failure point. The impact from the semi hitting the rear of the car shoved the seat into Sally's back, sealing her fate.

David refuses pain medication for his amazingly minor injuries, though he is stunned and shocked from the ordeal. Unable to stand without wobbling, he signs frantically to the nurse that he needs a wheel chair to go see his mother. Not knowing sign language, the nurse is bewildered. David shores up his strength and yells, in his near-perfect speech, "I want to see my mother!"

Rushing into the ER and frantic with worry, Dorothy Nickerson arrives and informs the staff she is Isaac's sister. Older than Isaac by about 15 years she is nonetheless spry and athletic from years of sailing and hiking through exotic archeological sites.

"Where is my family?" she demands. "I want to see them. Please tell me what happened."

After being briefed on everyone's condition, Dorothy insists she be able to accompany David to see his mother. With foreboding she maneuvers his wheel chair to the trauma room. At the sight of Billie's lifeless body on the gurney, violated by invasive tubes and intravenous lines, Dorothy is overtaken with grief. The hopeless rhythm of the ventilator makes her stomach turn and she is glad David cannot hear it.

Through the night and into the next day, Billie hovers between a machine-supported life and an irreversible death that will come when the machine is turned off. Despite the admonitions of the medical staff, that there is no brain activity, no hope of survival, Isaac cannot bear to remove life support.

"Not yet," he refuses. "We're not ready yet."

Vigilant through the interminable hours, David sits by his mother's side and demands that she live, that she not give up, that somehow, miraculously, she can will herself to return. He rises to his feet to move closer to her.

"Mom," he whispers. "I know you're in there. I know you can hear me. Come back to us. Just try harder. I know you can do it. You taught me everything I know - music, sign language - you taught me to never give up no matter what. Please, please. Don't give up now."

"Oh, David, don't."

"No, Aunt Dorothy. I won't stop. Mom can't stop trying. Tell her," he implores.

"It's too late. She's gone, David. She's gone."

The scream of the heart monitor pierces the air but it's the green flat line signifying his mother's death that pierces David's heart. He grabs his mother's hand desperately.

"No! Mom, if you die I'll hate you forever! I'll never forgive you for leaving me!"

"Please, David. You don't mean that," Dorothy sobs. "You can't say goodbye when you're so angry."

Dorothy and an orderly force David back to his wheelchair and re-move him from the room as he pounds furiously on the arm of the chair.

You didn't tell me he would hate me! Please bring me back so I can explain!

It's too late, Billie. We can't bring you back. This was the deal. Your life for David's soul, for his gifts to the world.

There must be a way...

No, dear. Come now. There are important things for you to do. You'll see. It was meant to be. You cannot hesitate or there will be consequences for all of you.

Outside, the fog has lifted to reveal twilight, Billie's favorite time of day, when the setting sun tints the sky with red and purple ribbons that melt into an indigo curtain.

When her respirator is turned off, the blackness of unconsciousness dissolves into blue, white and golden light. Billie Nickerson stands on the threshold of a world where there is no pain, no sorrow, no regret, where the burdens of jealousy, pride and judgment are as light as air and lifted away into the ether.

Still, there are memories that float by swiftly like flotsam - early days as a happy child, adolescent insecurity, abandonment, love, loss - her conscious mind clearing the debris that would hold her back on her soul's journey. The annoying drone of a complex earthly existence segues into an echo of bells, soft bells like wind chimes, as she moves through the loosely-bound arms of a galactic cloud.

How peaceful, she thinks. *How loving. Is this where I belong?*

Unexpectedly, invisible hands pull her back trying to keep her earthbound. Her husband, son and daughter entice and plead with an energy so strong it is almost palpable. But a force much stronger attracts her and she is once again tranquil, bodiless, in a space beyond space. Welcoming souls who will initiate Billie and guide her to the hereafter appear. It seems as if they are all swimming, being carried along by a current they can't control, under the direction of someone or something indescribable.

Billie is caught in the flow, but she is compelled to turn back, to look one last time at her family, at their sorrow and anguish, and she vows to return, not realizing it could mean an eternity in limbo.

Chapter 1

20 Years ago - The Love Story

The Port Avalon University courtyard is alive with pop music on a bright June day. Job applicants chatter with anticipation at being interviewed by the town's most prestigious companies looking for the best and brightest graduate students. With commencement only two weeks away there is no time to waste for securing one's future, and every booth in the row of enticingly-designed exhibits has a line of students waiting their turn.

Isaac Nickerson, a Navy officer, stands in front of a recruiting booth at the far end of the row, speaking with pride and encouragement to the young men and women who show an interest in serving their country before going into the private sector.

A poster of an aircraft carrier navigating its way powerfully through the ocean adorns the booth emblazoned with the words: "Life, Liberty and the Pursuit of All who Threaten it."

"The education you have already received here at Port Avalon U will help you advance to officer status much quicker than if you enlisted with only a high school diploma," Isaac informs. "Unparalleled career opportunities, experiences, and challenges draw some of the brightest and most skilled people into the Navy – while helping others realize potential they may not even know they have. From the high-tech to the awe-inspiring, America's Navy offers careers and jobs that fit all backgrounds and interests. There are literally hundreds of distinct professional roles in dozens of exciting fields. And however you serve – as Enlisted or Officer, full-time or part-time – you'll find unrivaled training, support and experience in a career unlike any other."

Isaac continues full throttle to several intrigued students while some others peel away. "The most valuable asset to America's Navy is its people. Sailors represent the best and brightest that America has to offer. And the Navy's commitment to their well-being is reflected in their benefits package, training opportunities, and life-changing world travel."

An obtrusive chant of "No more war! No more war!" grows louder and closer. A group of demonstrators carrying signs enters the courtyard and stops right in front of Isaac's station.

The signs are colorful but ominous: "We can bomb the world to pieces, but we can't bomb it to Peace" and "When the Rich wage WAR, it's the Poor who DIE."

At the front of the line is a girl who takes Isaac's breath away. Billie Donovan - he will soon learn is her name, with an unruly flowing mane of golden hair, a passionate demeanor and sonorous voice - stands out from the throng. With just one glance, his heart takes an unexpected turn from a firm allegiance to the military to be willing to die for this woman, the goddess Eirene come to earth, the personification of Peace.

Jesus, Isaac chastises himself. *Control yourself, man. She is mortal and you are a Navy Captain! And she's stealing your thunder.*

Excusing himself from the potential recruits, Isaac approaches the group and stands face to face with Billie. He raises his hands in an effort to quiet them down. Oddly enough they comply, but not without some complaining.

"Hey Dough Boy," one of them snickers. "Better stand down. We mean business and we have a right..."

Isaac exerts his formidable six-foot-two height. "Yes, you have a right. But first of all I'm not a doughboy. That's an infantryman from WWI. I'm a Navy Captain."

"With four stripes and a bar on your shoulder, no less," this feline-like vision needles him.

"And on my sleeve, as well," he parries, musing to himself that it should be his heart.

"Not to mention the Eagle on your collar." Billie Donovan patronizes Isaac with a devilish twinkle in her eyes that raises the hair on his neck. "They certainly stand out on your dress khakis."

"You seem to know a lot about uniforms for an antiwar girl." His probing dark eyes do not intimidate Billie.

"Well, I've seen my share of uniforms walking around downtown when a ship is in port. And I must say you cut an imposing figure, even if you are a war hawk."

Isaac finds it amusing that she is swathed in the uniform of the iconic flower child: peasant skirt and blouse, soft moccasins, an Indian headband forming a halo around her shoulder length hair. Appropriately, her right hand is raised in the two-finger sign of Peace. So young to be an anachronism.

"Hey, Billie. Quit the playing around with the enemy here. We've got a protest to continue." Impatient, the band of demonstrators starts to move on without her.

"Don't worry. I'm coming. Let's move to the administration office," Billie commands, and the group moves on, flashing signs and chanting, "No more war, No more war."

For one fleeting moment, Billie turns back to see Isaac's curious eyes still following her.

Later that afternoon, Isaac packs up the booth and recruiting documents, loads everything into his jeep and drives down to the university campus pub. He needs a cold one. Inside, the pub is buzzing with animated conversations of every stripe. He sits at the bar and heaves a weary sigh. It has been a long, hot day and the recruiting soliloquy became tiresome.

"I'll have whatever's on tap."

"Sure thing." The bartender lays the obligatory cocktail napkin on the bar along with a basket of mixed nuts.

"How about something to eat, like some crow?"

In the mirror behind the bar, Isaac sees that same head of unruly hair. He spins the stool around to face Billie Donovan head on. "Well, look who's here? The leader of the pack."

"Buy a peacenik a drink?" She invites herself to sit next to him.

"Shirley Temple?"

"Anything with rum in it."

"Are you even old enough to drink?"

"Seventeen for the next two hours, then I'm legal. But you're the first to question my age. The bartender doesn't care."

Isaac motions the bartender over and a drink for the lady is decided on.

"So how is it at 17, almost 18, that you are at the University already?"

"I'm a savant," she laughs. "Actually I graduated high school a year early and received a music scholarship." Billie sips her drink, a Mai Tai.

"Rum is a drink for old salts," Isaac says. "Are you a sea faring lass?"

"Who me? Not me. Haven't been on a boat since I was a kid. But I like to find creative ways to get my vitamin C. Cheers."

They clink glasses in *Salute* and both take a satisfying swallow.

"So, Navy man, what are you doing recruiting? Shouldn't you be at sea or something, off to the next combat mission?"

"Not me. I'm a nautical design engineer."

"Well, that's a bright light in the darkness here. Someone who creates instead of destroys. So why are you still in the Navy?"

"It's in my DNA. I come from generations of shipbuilders and seafarers. I wanted to learn the most modern technological advances in designing faster and more efficient ships, and the Navy offered the best opportunity."

"That's hard to believe, but if you say so."

"You're a snippy one, aren't you? And what are you all about? Besides disrupting the status quo?"

"Well, that's a story for another time. For now, I just want to kick back, erase the day from my mind, and enjoy some good company."

"Well, I'll drink to that." Isaac takes a solid swig.

"Hey, Billie, how about a tune?" someone yells across the bar.

"Yeah, tickle those ivories for us, Billie," another chimes in.

Soon the chant rises up, "Billie, Billie, Billie…"

"Okay, okay," Billie raises her arms to yield.

Isaac is intrigued. "You play piano?"

"Yeah, a little."

Billie sits herself down at the upright piano, and plinks on it a bit. "A little out of tune, but here goes. Any requests?"

"How about some Elton John?" The crowd laughs, enjoying the joke.

Attacking the keys with exuberance, Billie plays the opening bars of "Crocodile Rock," then finishes with a flourishing glissando. Instead of the applause one would normally hear at the end of a flamboyant performance, there is an anticipated silence. Everyone knows what is about to happen.

Deftly, gently, Billie segues from the rock and roll groove to a demonstration of musical "moonlight," Claude Debussy's *Claire de lune*, one of his most famous and recognizable compositions. Being one of the rare pieces in classical music to find its way numerous times into pop culture, it is also one of the most demanding for performers, requiring a sensitivity of touch that would not shatter the delicate and subtle colors of Debussy's writing.

The shimmering melody, marked *con sordina* - a soft muted approach - then grows in brilliance as it proceeds, with an octave passage in *rubato* tempo, leading to a new melody which Billie executes with even greater sublimity.

Familiar with Billie's stunning piano skills, the pub crowd listens with rapt attention and respect. For Isaac, there is something he has never felt before in his life. Something like love, but more than love. More like an out of body experience, not that he's ever had one. But there is this subconscious recognition that if angels could dance on the keyboard they would do so when Billie Donovan plays.

Cheers and Bravos follow Billie back to her seat at the bar. A fresh Mai Tai is waiting for her.

Isaac is speechless. All he can do is stare at this amazing young woman sitting next to him who is at once naive and knowing, and a cultured musician to boot.

"Well, say something," she challenges in that teasingly sardonic tone of hers. "Never heard anyone play the piano before?"

"Not like that. Never like that."

A few drinks later, Isaac and Billie walk back to her dorm. The sexual tension is palpable, like that of a movie romance where the heat emanates from the screen without so much as a touch between the two leads. Gentleman that he is, Isaac restrains himself from taking her in his arms right there on the courtyard. In turn, Billie moves away coyly then drifts closer to him. In a dance of courting, they never say a word, but every time their eyes lock, the message is clear.

"Well, here I am," Billie announces when they arrive. "Will I see you again, before you are deployed, or something?"

He smiles at the idea. "I don't get deployed. But I do leave tomorrow for an assignment in D.C."

"Oh. Well, I guess this is it then. It was nice to meet you and get a little drunk with you."

"Drunk with fascination, I think. Yes. But if it's okay, I'll call you when I get back. Now that you're legal."

"How long?"

"About a month or two, I think."

"I'd like that…if you remember me by then."

"Believe me, Billie Donovan, I could not forget you."

"In that case, Captain Nickerson, you may call."

Billie hands him her personal card and he slips it into his shirt pocket. Isaac watches her enter the dorm then turns to walk away, unfulfilled desire overtaking his senses. But moments later, he hears his name being called from a third story window. He turns his eyes upward to see Billie standing there in the window, beckoning him to come up.

Chapter 2

"Get a move on, Billie! We're going to be late." Austin nudges her along as he invites himself into her dorm room.

"I'm coming, I'm coming," Billie assures him. She stuffs her music sheets into an already overstuffed carry bag. "We have plenty of time before rehearsal begins."

They arrive at the auditorium green room to find the other orchestra members commandeering their spaces. "Don't worry," one of them informs, "rehearsal has been pushed up to 6 o'clock. The conductor is still *en route*."

Billie and Austin find an empty cubby in the wall case and put their music and belongings in.

"In that case, I'm going to stroll through the festival for awhile," Billy decides. "Want to come?"

Austin shakes his head, "No. I've got to go over this one part in the music that I can't seem to master."

"Okay. I'll be back soon. You'll be great tonight. Don't worry."

Outside the concert hall, several aisles of exhibits and booths color the campus courtyard adding to the ambience of the Port Avalon U Arts Festival. Billie grabs a quick sandwich and a drink from one of the food kiosks and munches while she strolls. One tent catches her eye.

"Tarot Card Readings by Dorinda" the sign reads, "Truth Seekers Welcome."

"Hmm. Why not. I've got a few bucks to splurge."

Billie pulls the faux velvet curtain back on the tent and walks inside. The music of flute, wind chimes and celeste infuse the air with an ethereal lightness. A small square table is covered with a ruby red cloth, several decks of cards, and an intriguing crystal ball that seems to glow with life.

"Hello? Is anyone here?" Billie wonders where the gypsy, or whatever she is, could be. The tent is as small as a closet.

As though an apparition, she appears, dressed in a beautiful blue kaftan and a gorgeous gold and red head wrap that accentuates her startling green eyes.

"I'm Dorinda. Welcome. Please have a seat."

Billie obliges.

"What can I do for you today?" Dorinda's voice is melodic and lilting.

"Uh - I just thought a general 'how's my life' kind of reading for now."

"Do you have a special problem or issue you would like clarified for you?"

As fascinated as Billie is with the paranormal she knows that some mediums are fakes and try to extract information from their marks by asking what seem to be benign questions but are quite revealing. So, she hedges.

"Maybe you can see something that I can't."

"Well, we'll start with that and perhaps other deeper issues will come to light."

Dorinda places three decks of cards on the table, each with distinct and beautiful art designs denoting their themes: Mystical Oracle cards inspired by Gods, Goddesses, Angels and Spirit Guides; Vibrational Energy cards denoting positive and healing energies through impressionistic art; and the Rider-Waite Tarot with brilliant drawings of Major and Minor Arcana figures and symbols.

"Take each deck separately and shuffle them, then place the decks face down on the table side by side."

Billie does as asked.

Dorinda sets two decks aside and fans the first deck across the table.

"Take a deep breath and without any forethought choose the first three cards from anywhere in the deck, and lay them face down."

Again, Billie does as asked.

The ritual is repeated with the other two decks until nine cards are laid across the table, three in a row.

"This is a lot of shuffling," Billie jokes.

"We do this so it is your energy in the cards and not mine. I will now pick one card from each row to give you an idea of who you are and what is happening in your life."

Dorinda turns over Card 1.

"The Judgement card. You are a person of good intentions, quite motivated and believe you can do anything you set your mind to."

"Oh, that's good. Isn't it?"

Dorinda smiles at Billie's uncertainty.

"I see by the second card, The Moon, that you have an impulsive spirit and are quite independent."

"Isn't every woman these days?"

"Not every," Dorinda remarks. "But you are also fickle and some-times very difficult to know. On the other hand you are mysterious which adds to your charm. This can be beneficial as you have recently had a romantic liaison with a new man. Or, it could be the ruination of a relationship."

One of Billie's eyebrows raises, her antennae now up.

"You are polar opposites," Dorinda continues. "He is a bit older than you, quite disciplined and serves his country, while you are respectful of him but totally antiwar."

Billie's jaw drops open. "How did you - ?"

"Correct?"

"Yes, I have to admit you're correct."

"Now, the Hermit card shows you are separated right now by dis-tance but not for long. He will return and you will renew your friend-ship. It will grow quite strong very soon. But I see some obstacles, some very powerful forces against this union that you must fight."

"Fight who? How?" Billie surprisingly feels a trust building up for this woman who could possibly determine her future.

"Let us look." Turning to her crystal ball Dorinda moves her hands lightly and elegantly over the orb, absorbing its ethereal energy.

Finally, she pronounces, "Time will resolve all things."

"That's it?" Billie snaps. "Time will resolve all things? I've got this supposedly great relationship with a man who, if he had any sense would avoid me, and there are very powerful forces standing in the way. How will it be resolved? When?"

"I see patience is not one of your virtues," Dorinda replies, patiently. "Fate has its own time table. Well, my time with you is up, my dear."

"But I have so many questions. You can't stop now. I want to see you again. How long will you be here?"

Dorinda stands to signal the end of the reading, and takes Billie's hand in hers. "As long as you need me, I will be here."

The warmth and strength of Dorinda's hand pulsates through Billie's body, startling her with its power.

Billie exits the tent but the sensation of Dorinda's essence still lingers, even as Dorinda the Mysterious dematerializes into the crystal ball.

Chapter 3

Billie counts the days on the calendar. When she surpasses 45 she panics.

"Oh, crud. Oh, bloody crud," she groans. "No, no, no. I can't be."

Pregnancy is not in her schedule at this point in her life. And no way to begin a relationship with a man so conventional as Isaac Nickerson, especially since she and Isaac never even slept together that magical night.

Feeling irritated and rejected by a man she had only spent a few hours with, who had resisted her self-indulgent seduction, she foolishly succumbed to a drunken fling with the pub's bartender who must have put some kind of aphrodisiac in her drink. She can never tell Isaac what an idiot she was.

What am I thinking? she admonishes herself. It's been almost six weeks and Isaac still hasn't returned from D.C. He has called only once and all he left was a vague voice mail message. *Maybe he won't come back at all. Then he will never know. I won't have to tell him. I can handle this alone if I have to. Yes. I'll do it alone.*

* * *

The Port Avalon summer concert series under the stars has attracted a standing-room only crowd. The most talented and gifted local musicians are featured, with Billie as the star performer. Thundering applause greets her as she takes the stage and sits at the gleaming white Steinway.

Billie knows better than to let her emotions cloud her focus for the music. All attention, all energy must be centered on the keyboard, on the page, on the divine meaning of Beethoven's Moonlight Sonata.

Legend tells it that by the time Beethoven played the Sonata in public his loss of hearing was well into its advanced stages, so he was known to play it louder than one typically would. Not so the pianists who followed him and made Moonlight Sonata a timeless romantic classic.

Including Billie. She learned early in her studies that to be an artistic pianist is to feel that a breeze just came through a window to speak to your music and sets lightly on your fingers as you play. To develop a laser focus on a composition is to know a loneliness that is crowded with the beautiful. To believe that each interpretation represents a new song to the universe - the harmony of the angels, that can alter the celestial consciousness.

Standing on a hill out of her range of sight is Isaac, who listens with his entire being, tears streaming silently down his face at the splendor of her performance. He knows then that Billie was meant to be a part of his life, his one and only love, his reason for being. She is his song. But could he ever be hers? Is he worthy? Could he ever give her anything close to what her music gives her? Was that first night that they met just a dream, a fantasy? Should he have taken advantage of the obvious sexual heat between them and, once invited to her dorm room, taken advantage of her uninhibited playfulness?

Isaac's Washington, D.C. assignment had sent him unexpectedly to battle-torn countries to retrieve injured victims, mostly children, and bring them back to the ship to receive medical treatment. Witnessing the horrors of war once again impacted him more than ever, and Billie's words kept resounding in his head. As proud as he was of serving his country Isaac realized he could no longer be part of the problem; he wanted to be part of the solution, to find another way to serve. And he wanted Billie by his side, to be his moral compass. But he had been gone six weeks and had called her only once in all that time.

Maybe she won't even want to see me. He is discouraged by the thought. *Maybe she has found someone else.*

Nevertheless, he is bound and determined to reconnect and to win her heart. Courting Billie Nickerson will be tricky. She is not one to be manhandled. He will take it slow, introduce her to the things he loves, open himself completely to her and take the risk that she can see in him a man who will devote his life to her but will also let her march to her own drummer.

* * *

Billie answers the phone in an agitated voice. She hopes it's not that bartender who keeps trying for a replay of their besotted one-night stand. Surprised to hear his voice, Isaac's voice, she stutters, "Oh - oh, it's you. I hadn't expected to hear from you again." *No, I was dying to hear from you again, you typical male who says he'll call and then doesn't!*

"I'm so sorry, Billie. I was on an assignment that didn't allow for personal phone calls. But I did think about you all the while I was gone. Will you forgive me enough to see me, maybe for coffee or a drink?

"Well..." She wants to play hard to get but easy to forgive. "I'm pretty busy these days with rehearsals and such. But I think I can find some time to get together. Just for coffee, mind you."

Billie hangs up the phone thanking her lucky stars that she is not pregnant. Just a late period. It's not the first time nature disrupted her body's rhythm which, for a girl whose life revolves around time and tempo, seems an illogical physical flaw. But if the unthinkable had happened, terminating the pregnancy would be her only option.

Dorinda's cryptic premonitions about the obstacles to her relationship with Isaac caused her to ruminate about her fate if she had an abortion. Would she have to keep it a secret forever? Could she? Or would she break under the pressure and confess it to Isaac in the spirit of full disclosure, thus giving impetus to the powerful forces Dorinda warned of that would tear them apart?

No, she decided, the gods had not meant her to bear a philandering bartender's baby conceived in a moment of irresponsible lust. So she had made an appointment with a clinic. Thankfully, she did not have to keep it.

* * *

Through the ensuing months, Billie and Isaac enjoy easy dates and movies and intellectual conversations. But they fight and debate constantly. *She* is hesitant to get serious about a man who devotes his life to the military even if it's just to build ships, and *He* can't understand her relentless acrimony toward the military, against men and women who sacrifice so much for home and country. Until one day Billie explodes with repressed rage over an excruciating personal loss.

"She was just an impressionable, idealistic kid then. What did she really know about any of it. My own sister, shot to death by armed guards firing on student anti-war protesters," Billie rants. "Violent anarchists infiltrated the peaceful group and she was caught in the fray and got killed for it."

So that's it. The root of her angst. Isaac empathizes with her pain, for he lost his own brother to a land mine in a Godforsaken corner of the earth. *What did he know about war? He was just a kid...*

Her sister's death inspired Billie to pacifism. It was Isaac's brother's death that affirmed his pledge to the Navy. Now things seem tinged with gray, no longer black and white. But he and the woman he was falling in love with were still worlds apart on this issue.

"Billie, if this relationship is going to work we have to agree to disagree about some things. Let's build on the things we agree on."

"You're right, Isaac. We'll move forward and never look back. I want a whole new life with you, new experiences, new memories."

"I know the perfect place to start."

Chapter 4

Billie's first sailing experience on Isaac's sleek sailboat thrills her. She hasn't been on the water since she was a child, and never on such an exquisite vessel. The wind on her face, the invigorating mist of salt water are luxurious sensations breathing new life into her soul. Something mysterious and grand is happening to her and all her rigid ideas about life and politics and class identity drift away with the breeze.

Second to the thrill of sailing with Isaac is the feeling of veneration when she visits the Nickerson home. The structure itself - a towering Victorian, all white with a bright red roof and shutters - is a home Billie could only dream of as a child. Climbing the steps to the front door fills her with anticipation and not a little dread. She, too, comes from a family of seafarers, but none so esteemed as the Nickerson clan.

Scanning the parlor, Billie can truly see the home's history. It is filled with functional antiques, sturdy furnishings handed down from generation to generation and still used proudly. Artistic memorabilia and artifacts, collected by the Nickerson family during centuries in the business of designing sailing ships, line the shelves of the oak wood breakfront and mahogany table tops.

An impressive Nickerson Coat of Arms hangs proudly over the fireplace. The crest is blue, with two ermine bars; and on a silver chief there are three gold suns.

"The family motto, Per *Castra ad astra*, means Through the Camp to the Stars," Isaac tells her.

"I am in awe," Billie says. "Humbled, actually, by you and your family."

Sounding now like a museum curator, Isaac continues with, "The name Nickerson is an ancient Anglo-Saxon surname that came from the personal name Nicholas. The Latin form of this name was Nicolaus, and it was derived from the Greek name *Nikolaos*, which is derived from the words *nikan*, meaning"to conquer," and *laos*, which means 'people.' However, the name is best remembered by an American corruption of this name: Santa Claus."

Billie can't help but laugh at his uncommon humor. "Oh, Isaac. Thank you for trying to make me feel comfortable. I love Santa Claus. I mean, you know, the symbolism -"

Yes, she is falling in love with him, she admits to herself - his solid strength, his pragmatic demeanor, a tall, dark and handsome knight on a white horse, the total opposite of her will-o'-the-wisp personality.

They walk through the house and Billie feels both warmth and cool breezes. Eerie. Isaac says it's just the changing sea air but the spooky feeling follows her like a shadow.

From a second floor veranda at the back of the house, Billie can see the family cemetery. A century of generations is buried there just steps away from a cliff jutting out proudly into the ocean. Nearby, a large expanse of ground lies yet untouched, waiting patiently for the remaining Nickersons to come. Over the white picket fence that neatly edges the cemetery, the ocean surf below swirls and splashes against the sea wall, a whirlpool of conflicting emotions.

Billie is enchanted with the house and its proximity to the ocean. Her grandfather and father had labored on the fishing wharfs and boatyards by an upstate river, while she existed in a neighborhood of wall to wall cement and blacktop freeways, with barely a tree-filled park let alone the open sea. Being able to come to Port Avalon to study music in earnest at the conservatory was a breath of fresh air, sea air, and it enlivened her. And now, this house, this man, this fantasy life is within her grasp.

"Continuing my family heritage is one of the reasons I want to be a ship designer," Isaac explains, bringing Billie back to reality, "to bring all of their historic innovations into the modern era."

"I can understand that now that I've seen this wonderful house, so alive with memories and the riches of the past."

"This can be your house, too," Isaac suggests. "It needs a modern woman's touch, as well as her breathtaking music."

"What are you saying, Isaac?"

"I'm asking you to marry me, Blanche Donovan. To be Blanche Nickerson."

Blanche Donovan. She cringed whenever anyone called her that.

"When I was a little girl, I was constantly teased about my name. Blanche. It's something you do to a pot of vegetables until their skins fall off."

"But Blanche also means white and shining – like a pure light of inspiration," Isaac sermonizes.

"I'm not an angel yet." Her broad smile reveals slightly imperfect teeth and childlike dimples. "Billie is more like me. Good old down to earth Billie Donovan."

"Then marry me Billie Donovan."

"But you're still in the Navy. What if you are assigned to some other city or another country? Then what?"

"Actually, my term of service is up in a few months. I'll be back in Port Avalon permanently, and this house will always be my home. I want you to share it with me. What do you say?"

Flustered and taken off guard all Billie can say is, "I - I don't know..."

"We've been dating almost a year now, Billie. What's wrong? Do you have reservations about me? Is there something you want to know? Or is there something you're not telling me?"

Yes, I had a fling with a bartender while you were gone, and thought I was pregnant, wanted to have an abortion, but thank God I didn't have to. That little bit of information will forever remain unsaid.

And what about those frightening dreams and visions about a child who follows her like a shadow that have come out of nowhere and are with her constantly? Are they just the product of her guilt? And why should she feel guilty about something she only thought about? How can she possibly share this bizarre behavior with Isaac and still have him think she is sane?

"Reservations about you, no, but about me. I'm not sure what I could offer this marriage, if I am mature enough or worthy enough to have all of this and you, too. I think - oh, gosh. I have to consult my psychic." Billie breaks the seriousness with a nervous laugh.

"Consult your - psychic? Uh - you're joking. That wit of yours always throws me."

"Would you take back your proposal if I told you I believe in psychics and Tarot cards and such?"

"You mean fortune tellers?"

"Well, kind of. I mean no one can really predict the future, but maybe they can tell us what kind of luck or providence we will experience. It kind of gives us some insight and a little hope."

"The only hope we have is hard work and accepting our lot in life. There are no amulets to protect us from harm, and no talismans to bring us good luck. But if, and I mean *if* there are such things then you are my good luck charm. And I need you."

She nestles deeply into his arms, feeling safe and secure. Yet something unsettling still quivers within her. Dorinda's warnings, the ghostly feeling that follows her through every room, the fear that some ominous power will tear them apart, makes her hesitate.

Holding Isaac off with, "I need a little more time," Billie decides she must have another card reading.

* * *

In haste as on a mission, Billie finds her way back to the tent where Dorinda first read her cards. She is frantic to find, however, that Dorinda is not there. A different card reader sits quietly at the table with decks of cards and the crystal ball at her reach.

"Where's Dorinda? I really need to see her. She knows me."

"It's all right, my dear. We are all interconnected here. Whatever you gleaned from Dorinda's readings will be evident in my reading today."

Hesitant, but also desperate for clarity, Billie agrees. "I'm having strange dreams, visions, too. And they frighten me."

"Well, then, let us use some healing crystals first to calm you so we have a clear channel." The nameless woman with a kind face and sunny demeanor presents some large crystals and surrounds the Tarot cards with them. There are deep blue, rose, white and green stones of unique shapes and sizes, all meant to bring a meditative quietness to Billie's mood.

Nameless chooses a deck of cards and shuffles them, lays out a few before Billie, then turns them over one by one.

"The Archangel Gabriel. He is the Angel of Communication and the Arts, inspiring you into creative pursuits. I understand you are a gifted pianist."

"I - yes, I am," Billie replies with humility. Her eyes open wide involuntarily. "How did you know that?"

"It's all in the cards, my dear. Your cards."

"Oh. Right."

"This talent will serve you well in the future."

"I hope so. I want to play professionally, in a symphony one day."

"Perhaps. But it seems to turn in a different direction than you aspire to."

"I'm not sure I like that," Billie pouts.

"The Archangel Gabriel also guides hopeful parents in fertility and child conception."

"Billie gasps. "Yes! The visions are about a child...but they are unclear. I don't know what the dreams mean. They just frighten me."

"Your musical talent will serve you well here. And your child, when it comes, will also be so inclined, for you will teach it to this new soul. It is vital that you do so. Even from outside the womb music vibrations nurture. Gabriel will be there to guide you as to what to do."

"God, I hope so. I'll need all the help I can get."

"Ah, Caution," the woman reveals the next card. "You are sometimes impulsive and quick to act or react."

Yeah, like that fling I'm trying to forget. Billie shivers at the thought.

"But now, you feel hesitant to move forward with a decision, a very serious one, it seems."

"Yes. The man I am seeing wants to marry me. And I so want to marry him. But these dreams make me apprehensive, as though something will ruin it."

"Just breathe into it and when you make your decision everyone concerned will flourish."

"Ha. Just like that." Billie snaps her fingers. "Sorry," she apologizes for being cheeky. "But it can't be that simple."

"Take time to fully consider the situation, take small steps and you will soon find things falling into place."

"Yes, I did tell him I needed more time."

"Then use the time wisely."

Billie is stumped. "How will I do that?"

"This card, the Knowing card, tells you to listen to what you hear and act upon the messages you receive. They will guide you on the journey you are destined for."

Billie huffs in exasperation. "This is all so cryptic. I'm just not that evolved on metaphysical things. If I'm to have all this help, all these guides, why do I feel so afraid, so panic-stricken?"

"Let us pull a card from a different deck."

Billie cries out when the Death card is turned over. "Oh, my God. What does that mean? Am I going to die? Is my child going to die?"

"Soon you will have a dream, or perhaps a visitation, in which someone or something threatens to harm you, even kill you. You will try to escape or fight back."

"Kill me! Why? What have I done?"

The reader is quiet now, weighing her words carefully. "Both you and your child are in danger. It is not imminent but it hovers like a black cloud."

"Danger? What kind of danger?" Billie is hyperventilating now, despite being surrounded by healing music and crystals. "Pick another card. Please!"

"Your final card, The Chariot. Your child will face great peril but his life will also be heroic. He -"

"What are you talking about? It's not even real. I can't tell in my visions if it's a girl or boy - it's a *he*?"

"Yes."

Billie is elated to know she could one day have a son, Isaac's son. He will be strong and wise just like his father. But then she remembers the danger part and her emotions burst forth begging for clarification.

"Your boy will possess something that others covet and are willing to die for, and kill for."

Through her tears Billie pleads, "What could he possibly possess - what *will* he possess that is so ominous? A - a golden rattle for heaven sake?!"

"I'm not yet clear on the prophecy. This is some time in the distant future, but I feel it will be something of great importance to him, your family, and perhaps the world."

Overwhelmed, Billie tries to disavow the premonition and rises to leave in haste. But as a parting warning, Nameless implores Billie to heed her words, to take the Tarot seriously.

After the curtain closes behind Billie, Nameless turns to the crystal ball wherein Dorinda's hologram resides and talks to her.

"Are we certain this girl is up to the challenges she will face, Dorinda?"

"She will struggle and resist," Dorinda concedes, "and the dark spirits will push her to her limit. But if she focuses on the end result - the destiny of her child - she will prevail. She has one personal trait that she can pass on to her son, one that they will share through many lifetimes: her divine musical gift and its unbounded capacity to raise and change the consciousness of mankind."

"But not just any music, I assume."

"No. Not just any." Dorinda is emphatic on this point. "The music of the soul. Few can hear it, but her son will. He must."

"This is crazy," Billie tells herself as she tries to come to terms with the nameless Tarot card reader's forewarning about a son yet to be conceived and about the ominous fate that lies ahead for him.

"I just have to shift my thinking to something rational. Maybe in loving Isaac I'll adopt his sane way of looking at life. Maybe that's what I need. Someone rational. Someone who can talk me out of all this premonition nonsense."

Chapter 5

As a wedding present and as a way to give her own personal touch to the Nickerson house, Billie gifts Isaac with a mariner's bell, a symbol of the blending of their two families. The bell had come from a vessel her father and grandfather helped build. "What an incredible coincidence that your family was in the ship building business," Isaac remarks, admiring the vintage treasure.

"Yes, they were. But not as prosperous as your family. Fishing boats were their specialty, but they were quite sea worthy and sailed to many exotic ports."

As Billie polishes the brass bell to a gleaming finish, she reminisces about all the exciting adventures her father spoke of. She can pretend he is still alive, rocking in his favorite chair by the crackling glow of the fireplace with her devoted mother sitting nearby. And she can pretend he hadn't lost his business to an arsonist who burned his boatyard to the ground, and her parents with it.

* * *

On the eve of their wedding, Billie is in a beautiful suite of rooms on the third floor getting dressed for the rehearsal dinner. She wanted to design and sew the dress herself but, being a failure as a dressmaker, shopping was her only option and a lot more fun. She smoothes the turquoise blue dress down over her slim hips, feeling like a beauty from a bygone era. The antique design has a lace-paneled bodice bursting with beautiful deco beads, atop an ornate skirt that swirls and slinks to knee length. Wide, beaded tank straps hug Billie's smooth shoulders. It's no wonder she feels ready to dance the night away.

Admiring her image Billie twirls to imaginary music, humming a favorite waltz. Shockingly, an image appears behind her in the mirror - ghostly, not man or woman - and the phantasm causes Billie to stop mid-turn. Terrified, she backs away hastily and nearly trips over the ottoman at the foot of her bed. She grabs onto the bedpost and tries to hide behind it. Her scream is just a lump in her throat gagging her to silence.

"There is grave danger if you marry Isaac Nickerson." The voice seems to come from nowhere, certainly not from the unidentifiable apparition that hovers before her. Now it's above her, below her, and even inside her head.

"That's it," she tells herself. "I'm just hearing a voice in my head. That's it. No one is here. No one is here. Go away!" she commands the spirit. "You are not here. You don't belong here." The image disappears at her firm command, as though a light switch has suddenly turned it off.

Billie is shaken to her core. Her hands and forehead are sweaty with fear. Her heart races violently and she feels the dankness build up inside her beautiful dress. She runs to the bathroom, slips the shoulder straps down and douses her chest and underarms with cool water. Delicately, to not disturb her makeup, she blots the perspiration from her face and hairline. Resolutely she slows down her breathing to normal.

"Get a grip, Billie. Guests are arriving. You don't want them to think you're certifiable."

The festive music of violin, cello and flute performed by Billie's music colleagues emanates throughout the house, complementing the celebratory nature of the impending wedding of Billie Donovan and Isaac Nickerson.

Joyful and friendly hugs and kisses greet her as she descends the stairs, and Billie feels herself calming down to appreciate the moment.

Spotting an intriguing woman across the room, Billie approaches her and introduces herself.

"Oh, yes. I know who you are," Dorothy says with an amiable smile. "Isaac has sent me some photos of the two of you."

"Oh, how nice," Billie replies, thinking she is just a friend of her future husband. "You look very familiar, exotic in a way, but with your gorgeous white hair, you're not like Asian or anything, but look kind of like a gypsy card reader I met at the Port Avalon festival last summer. I mean, not that you're dressed in costume like her, but it's your green eyes and your aura...." Billie rambles, feeling like an idiot who lets stupid words tumble from her mouth.

"Oh, really?" Dorothy is truly amused. "You see fortune tellers? It's okay dear. I do, too. And I sometimes dress up for the Port Avalon festivals and work with crystals to give readings. Of course, I have no powers of foresight. It's just a lot of fun. Something I picked up on one of my trips to the Mediterranean."

Isaac strides over. "I see you've met my sister, Dorothy."

"Your sister! Oh, great. You must think I'm daffy."

Isaac is bewildered. "What happened?"

"Nothing, just girl talk. It's wonderful to meet you, Billie. I should have introduced myself." Dorothy takes Billie's hand in hers.

The energy from the woman's hand startles Billie and she stares blankly, openmouthed, at the familiar feeling.

"Dorothy has just returned from another of her jaunts to a land far away," Isaac reports, waking Billie to the here and now.

"Oh, you're a world traveler." Billie remarks benignly, trying to sound normal.

"Actually, I'm a digger."

"A what?"

"I go on archeological digs with some historians who humor their not-so-scientific buttinsky friend. I look for amulets and treasures to bring home."

"Rocks," Isaac needles Dorothy. "Just plain old rocks."

"As you can see, my brother has no time for such things. But he is quite attached to our father's watch fob. Thinks it brings him good luck."

"That's different. It's a family heirloom with a lot of tradition behind it," Isaac counters. "This fob is the only heirloom Father was able to leave me after years of giving his blood, sweat and tears to Fischbacher Shipping. I am fond of it, but I certainly don't consider it a lucky piece, not in the least."

"Fischbacher Shipping?" Billie interjects. "Where you just signed on as a designer?"

"Yes, in fact," Isaac says. "It's the only place in town that has the wherewithal to build the kind of ships I want to design."

"Nathan Fischbacher's company?" Dorothy grimaces. "Surely you didn't have to resort to working for that snake, Isaac."

"Thanks for the well wishes." Isaac makes no attempt to hide his disappointment.

"Oh, Isaac. Of course, I wish you well. He's lucky to have you. But tell him if he messes with my brother, he'll have me to contend with."

Isaac kisses Dorothy on the cheek and excuses himself. "Sorry, but I've got some guests to attend to. Coming Billie?"

"I'll be along, Isaac. I want to visit with Dorothy for a few minutes."

"What's this about Nathan Fischbacher?" Billie asks with concern after Isaac walks away. "Why do you dislike him so much?"

"It's a long story, but there has been bad blood between our families for years. Nathan's father and ours went at each other tooth and claw more than once about the industry's place in Port Avalon. We thought when old man Fischbacher croaked things would be different. But the apple doesn't fall far from the tree and Nathan, Jr. proved to be as self-serving as Nathan, Sr."

"Why would Isaac want to work for him, then?"

"Well, it's as he said," Dorothy explains. "Fischbacher Shipping is now the only game in town and Isaac would never leave Port Avalon to work elsewhere."

"I have faith in Isaac," Billie says, "and I'm sure you do, too. So we'll both watch out for him."

"You bet we will. And it won't hurt to call on my own good luck charms now and then." They both laugh, taking the edge off.

"So, did you bring any back this time?" Billie's curiosity about the occult now resurfaces. "Any new treasures or amulets?"

"Yes, some crystals, very powerful ones. When you have time, I'll show them to you."

* * *

Billie can't believe she is up for all this pomp and circumstance. After all, she's just out of her Bohemian phase, her Flower child persona that Isaac fell in love with. Is she just going along with this big blowout of a wedding to please him or is she really enjoying the elegance and history of it all?

On the advice of the most coveted wedding planner in town, Billie agreed to a wedding theme in keeping with the charm of the Nickerson's Victorian home, while at the same time paying homage to the seaside town of Port Avalon. Isaac had said the house needed a woman's touch and what better time to bring out the antique lace and china teacups than their wedding day.

Invitations were crafted on smooth ivory paper and scripted in calligraphy. This prelude to the big day hinted that guests would attend a garden wedding on a sprawling, manicured lawn enhanced with freesia- and gardenia-laden trellises, and that the reception dinner tables would be set out with gilt-edged china and delicate rosebud centerpieces.

They are not disappointed.

On a summerlike October day the traditional wedding music of a Mendelssohn string quartet introduces the handsome couple as they walk down the aisle toward a wedding arch festooned with flowers, seashells and nautical flags, overlooking the shimmering ocean. Arm in arm Billie and Isaac enjoy the ooh's and ah's of the guests.

Billie's dress is a lovely ecru Chantilly lace bodice draped over robin's egg blue taffeta. The flowing chiffon skirt with a scalloped lace hem kisses the tops of Billie's satin shoes. A soft, short veil of golden pearl- encrusted blue tulle halos her golden blonde hair.

Isaac's dinner dress white uniform is impeccably pressed and pleated, as a final tribute to his years of service now ending. Billie smiles when she notices the chain from his father's watch fob hanging from inside the cropped jacket down to his pants pocket.

"Thought you didn't believe in good luck charms," Billie whispers.

"This is different. It's our wedding day. We need all the luck we can get."

In her satin bridal purse, Billie carries something borrowed and something blue: a Lapis Lazuli crystal Dorothy loaned her. Its deep, celestial blue is the symbol of royalty and honor, gods and power, spirit and vision. Billie wants so much to believe the myth about the gem is true, as she and her future son will need all the godly power they can muster.

Around her neck she wears a glistening rose crystal pendant that Dorothy gifted to her because it carries musical vibrations - so appropriate for Billie. The something old: a pair of golden pearl earrings that belonged to Isaac's mother, long ago handed down to Isaac to give to his fiancée as a wedding present.

At the close of a lively reception, Billie throws her nosegay of pink roses over her shoulder to a shrieking and happy single girl, then she and Isaac bid the guests farewell. Upstairs they change into clothes suitable for a moonlit night on Isaac's sailboat.

They try to make light of the fact they are both orphans with no father to give away the bride and no mother to cry happy tears over "losing" her son.

"We have each other, Billie," Isaac says tenderly to his new wife. "We are all the family we need."

"For now," Billie replies. "Let's enjoy each other." *As long as we can, she thinks to herself. Until the premonition comes true: a son with gifts to give the world and powers that people will want to kill him for.*

Chapter 6

Billie glides through the surf with graceful arms, face up doing back-strokes in a meditative rhythm. It's almost twilight, just before the sun fully sets on the horizon, her favorite time of day. There is not a soul on the beach on this unseasonably warm April day. Isaac is at work and will be for a few more hours. Neighbors have finished their afternoon of sailing and boats are docked by the pier dozens of yards from where she swims. Even though she is six months pregnant, she never misses a day, not just to keep in shape but to give her boy - yes, it's a boy as predicted - an affinity with the ocean, its power and its serenity.

After several pregnancies and miscarriages, Isaac and Billie had all but given up hope that they would ever have a child. Disappointed, Isaac immersed himself in his work, trying to get Nathan Fischbacher to move into the futuristic era of shipbuilding and back his innovative designs. He is thrilled Billie's pregnancy has come this far but braces himself for another turn of fate.

Billie's goal of a PhD in music and a position on the staff of Port Avalon's Music Conservatory has come to fruition. But despite her accomplishments, deep inside she feels the miscarriages are her punishment for past indiscretions and for even considering preventing what might have been a magical child his chance to be born. Rationalizing that these unrealized children were not even meant to be, that the perfect child would be sent to her at the perfect time, she tucks her guilt away in a quiet place.

Now refreshed mentally and every muscle loosened and supple, Billie dries off in the cabana and changes clothes. Inside the house, she makes a cup of jasmine mint tea in the roomy kitchen to mellow her then sits at the grand piano by the garden doors.

"This calls for some Chopin," she decides and turns to her favorite piece, the E-*b* Major Nocturne, Op 9. She loves its elaborate and decorative tones and trills, which challenge her.

The classic piece opens with a legato melody, smooth and flowing. As Billie's left hand plays an unbroken sequence of eighth notes in simple arpeggios her right hand moves with fluidity in patterns of seven, eleven, twenty, and twenty-two notes. The nocturne is reflective in mood, softly romantic, until it suddenly becomes passionate. After a trill-like passage, the excitement subsides and the nocturne, as written, promises to end calmly.

Her hands moving deftly and elegantly on the keys, Billie is in a trance of her own manifestation. She has not missed one note of the melody that seems to float above seventeen consecutive bars of D-flat major chords. Near the end of the nocturne, however, her fingers voice a chord that Chopin had never written. Billie speaks an "Ouch" at hearing the discordant error.

"What the..."

She corrects the fingering and moves into the next phrase, but again the chord she strikes is not by her own doing. Her hands become rigid, her fingers spasm. A tritone chord is struck over and over. Billie shakes her fingers out and flexes her wrists, thinking she is more tired from the swim than relaxed. Disturbed but determined, she breathes deeply to begin again.

Instead, Billie screams, nearly falling off the piano bench, and tips over her tea cup. A ghoulish black cloud hovers over the keyboard. It has a voice, a creepy voice. "I've Got You Now," it sneers menacingly, and laughs with evil intent.

Billie pants and gasps from shock and fear. She swats at it as though it's a harassing, unwelcome bug, but her hand moves right through it. "What are you? Who are you?" She keeps trying to hit it to no avail.

"I'm your dark side, Billie. Everyone has one, even you. You can't escape me, especially in your music, because I am there in every note…in every Tritone chord…"

"Why are you doing this? Do I know you? What have I done to you? Please tell me."

"You'll find out soon enough, when you leave this nice little cocoon you've created for yourself and are at the mercy of death."

Billie slides off the bench and curls up on the floor in an effort to protect herself from an undeserved assault. "What? Are you going to kill me? Why? Please tell me."

That menacing laughter fills the room again, so loudly that Billie holds her ears to shut out the echo.

"Oh, I don't have to kill you. You'll do that quite well yourself. And next time we meet you'll understand the hell you've put me through."

Billie scrambles to her feet and backs out of the room as the dark cloud dissolves into its origins. She runs up the stairs to her bedroom, locks the door and buries herself beneath a pile of comforters, shivering with fright.

* * *

"What do the cards say?" Billie nearly shrieks hysterically, teetering on the edge of the chair, clawing at the red-clothed table. She is grateful that Dorinda has returned when she needs her more than ever, as though the enigmatic woman intuitively knew that her presence was required at this crucial time.

"First, they ask that you be calm, Billie. Your aura is a muddy brown, your energy is thick and dark with worry."

"Calm? How can I be calm when ghosts or black clouds or whatever are chasing me through the house, are sitting on my piano keyboard, are terrorizing me. I can hardly play a note of music without it going discordant, creating sounds that are not written on the page, that Mozart or Chopin would never write and I would never play!"

"And that is your key to survival," Billie. "To remember with your eyes, your mind, your fingers, your heart, the music that brings out the light in you and in the world, and chases away all the darkness. There is a reason that the music of the great Masters has lived on. Don't you recall that Mozart had his own demons that nearly destroyed his mind? Yet he prevailed in bringing forth the music of the Divine. That's what you must do. Fight the dark side. It has no power over you unless you let it."

"But why am I so terrified? I've been playing for years and years and have never felt this foreboding."

"The cards have told you what life has in store for you and your unborn child, the dangers as well as the rewards, and it's a great weight to have on your shoulders."

"It's more than a weight," Billie wails. "I'm not worthy of this - this - bringing forth a child that must help to save the world! I'm not Mary Mother of God! I'm just Billie Donovan."

"Dearest," Dorinda reassures her, taking Billie's trembling hand. "We are all just Billie Donovan in one form or another. But when life offers a challenge to us, we can't run away. We must face it head on or we never evolve, we never find our true purpose in life. Your challenge is beyond what most people have to confront, because the life and fate of another person is in your hands. Who else will teach him what he must know to fulfill his destiny? Only you, his mother. The woman who has known him in many lifetimes before and will know him in many lifetimes after this one."

"You ask too much." Billie lays her head down on her hands and sobs. "You ask too much."

"It is not I who asks," Billie. "It is the soul within you who has chosen this path, and who must walk it with your son."

* * *

With the aid of a large carafe of chamomile tea and sitting for hours in diffused mists of lavender oil, Billie wills herself to play softly on the piano only the most healing compositions. The works of Johann Sebastian Bach particularly soothe and refresh her psyche, her favorite being the Brandenburg Concertos.

For a time, Billie's life is back to normal. She can breathe easily. Her moods are more stable. Her time with Isaac is sweet and comforting. Most of all, her music is her solace and she regains authority over her technique and talent.

Billie even composes music now, and plays to her child in the womb. It's a joyous song, a lilting melody, with a rhythm that harmonizes with his heartbeats. She feels him grow stronger as she herself grows stronger. Without truly realizing it, Billie is playing his soul song, one he will remember when he needs it most. When his life is in full crisis. When she is no longer there to protect him.

* * *

"Billie, Billie! Wake Up!" Isaac cannot rouse her. She is deep into a nightmare that is the worst she has had. Holding her boy's head in her hands, she grabs at his ears, taking them for herself, leaving him without the ability to hear the sounds he needs to hear. She holds the ears in her hands, shuddering in horror. In their place are black holes on the sides of her boy's head. *How will he fend for himself? What have I done? What have I done?*

The screaming Billie hears is her own as she wakens to the reality of Isaac who is near hysteria himself.

"It's okay, Billie. Just a bad dream. I've got you now. You're safe."

The two of them hold each other for dear life, as Isaac rocks his wife back and forth into a state of calm and quiet.

"I'm so sorry, Isaac. So sorry to put you through this. How do you stand it? Aren't you sick of me?"

"Never. Whatever you're going through we can go through together. I'll always be here for you."

The stress and strain of the years of waiting for a child, the ominous premonitions of the Tarot, and the visions of evil that she has been experiencing take its toll, and Billie goes into premature labor.

"It's too soon," she cries. "I can't be in labor. I'm so sorry Isaac. It's my fault. All that swimming, the stress over my concert performances -"

"These things happen," the doctor tells them both. "It's not your fault, Billie. You are healthy and your baby is far enough along - more than seven months - to do quite well. I promise I'll take care of both of you."

But that chilling nightmare about "taking her boy's ears" fill her with dread. *Will my baby be born deaf? No he can't be. He'll be a musician, so he can't be deaf. He'll be fine. He'll be fine. He must be fine.*

* * *

David's birth is a miracle for Isaac and Billie. The son they thought they would never have was nurtured along by a recording of Billie's original music placed in his incubator, and after only a few weeks in the NICU he is now home, hearty and strong. For Billie, her work as a mother is just beginning, but hers will not be a normal motherhood.

She encourages Isaac that they name him David, "because he may have to grow up to slay dragons and giants," she teases, *knowing* that one day he may have to do just that. Isaac acquiesces gladly but for the pragmatic reason that having that name "makes you independent, resourceful, practical, and patient." A typical Isaac rationale.

For two years, Billie and Isaac are doting parents, content to have this one child who is everything to them. Except for fending off the ghosts that follow her everywhere, Billie remains strong and in control. She doesn't dare tell Isaac about these visitations, for he does not believe one iota in paranormal or metaphysical things. She has learned to compartmentalize and put them in their place where they cannot hurt her or her child. She wonders why they still hang around, why they don't just give up and bother someone else.

Then, miraculously, Billie is pregnant again, and this time a beautiful little girl is born. Sally is a bright and cheerful child, bouncy and perky. She attaches herself to her older brother, who takes on the role of her protector even at three years of age, a role he will fulfill all of his life.

Sally, the Princess, as Isaac calls her, is expert at wrapping him around her little finger from the time she is old enough to talk. She loves frilly dresses and dances around the room with abandon. To nurture this innate joy, Billie enrolls Sally in dance class and the unusually-coordinated toddler takes to it as if dancing is in her DNA.

As is his calling, David is fascinated with the piano. He sits next to Billie on the bench rapt and eager every time she plays. Soon, David is able to mimic Billie's fingering almost perfectly. Realizing he is a prodigy Billie coaches him to sight read every scale, every note, so that he masters not just what is on the page, but so he can hear the music in his head.

When he can entice David away from the piano, Isaac teaches his young son to sail. He can't play a note of music or talk about the art but bonds with his son through the nautical tasks of tying knots, hoisting sails and controlling the boat's wheel. David is a quick-study and Isaac is delighted that he takes to the intricacies of sailing so easily.

* * *

"Ahoy, there, Nickersons!" Dorothy climbs the front porch steps, eager to see her family. She has just returned from one of her digs, and is exhausted from the freighter cruise from a far side of the world to the welcoming sight of Port Avalon.

"Aunt Dorothy!" the children squeal, and shower her with hugs and kisses. They know she will have some exciting stories to tell.

"Oh, it's so good to see you both!" Dorothy flops on the couch with the two siblings cuddling next to her. "But first, I need to take off my shoes and wiggle my toes."

Billie and Isaac welcome Dorothy warmly and offer up a feast of real American food. "Oh, how I've missed good old home cooking," Dorothy gushes, relishing the familiar tastes. "Billie, you are almost as good a cook as you are a musician."

Billie laughs but won't take the credit. "Actually, it's Isaac who whipped up this delicious stew and even made the biscuits from scratch." Isaac does a seated bow acknowledging his wife's accolade.

"Well, I never thought my brother would slave over a hot stove. How did you get him to tear himself away from his drafting table long enough to learn?"

"Isaac has been a lot more domestic since he's become a father," Billie explains.

"And I love every minute of it," Isaac chimes in.

"How long are you visiting this time?" Billie asks.

"For as long as you will have me."

"Well, your room is still waiting for you, and I expect it will be a luxurious experience after living on a freighter and in huts and tents for so long."

"You bet it will be. I can't wait to hit that four-poster bed and rest my head on those down pillows."

"Aunt Dorothy," David implores, "you can't go to bed without hearing the new piece I learned."

"Wouldn't think of it."

"Good. Let's have coffee and dessert in the music room." Billie and Isaac clear the table as Dorothy and the children walk hand in hand to the 19th Century elegance of the room where the grand piano is the focal point, amidst comfortable couches and ottomans.

Dorothy thanks Billie for the coffee and delicious *petit four* and rests her feet on the ottoman while David seats himself at the piano. He is slightly built and the grand piano almost seems to diminish him further. Until he begins to play.

When David's fingers touch the keyboard he becomes larger than life. He performs his favorite music, McDowall's tenderly beautiful, "To a Wild Rose," with a confidence and sensitivity unusual for a seven-year old.

Unable to sit still, Sally pirouettes and glides in youthful elegance, complimenting her brother's music but not stealing the spotlight.

Dorothy smiles and applauds approvingly when they finish. "With David's music and Sally's dance abilities they make a great couple of performers, don't they?"

Isaac nods in agreement, trying to keep his pride in check. Billie's heart fills with joy for the moment, trying to keep at bay the thoughts of impending challenges and trials that await them all.

Chapter 7

"Billie! Dorothy!" Isaac calls out, frantic with fear. He carries a limp and delirious David into the house and lays him on the couch. "Call the doctor!"

"Isaac? For heaven's sake, what happened? What's wrong with David?" Billie holds her hand to David's brow. "He's burning up. Why?"

"I don't know." Isaac shakes his head. "We were on the boat and suddenly he started vomiting over the side. He got dizzy and almost fell overboard. I thought he was just seasick but David has never gotten seasick."

"The doctor will be here soon," Dorothy assures them after placing the call. "Maybe it's just some kind of flu. Is it going around school?"

"Not that I've heard," Billie answers. "He seems a bit delirious or confused. That's not a flu symptom."

"We need to get him to the hospital," Doctor McMillan recommends after checking David's vitals and symptoms.

"The hospital!" Billie and Isaac are alarmed. "Is it that serious?"

"I think he might have meningitis, but I can't be sure without some labs."

Exhaustive tests are run, samples of David's blood and cerebrospinal fluid are collected and rushed to the lab.

"How he contracted Meningitis is difficult to say, but I think we caught it early enough that a good dose of antibiotics can prevent it from worsening," Dr. McMillan reports. "I'll want all of you tested just in case, even though you have no symptoms at present."

"Of course, Doctor." Isaac, Billie and Dorothy agree without hesitation.

"We need to observe him for a few days and see how he's progressing."

Over the next weeks David seems to improve. The nausea subsides, his vertigo is sporadic and waning. But a new troubling symptom gives cause for alarm.

"Why are you holding your ear, David?" Isaac asks.

"It has a funny sound, Dad. It won't go away."

"What kind of funny sound? Can you describe it?"

"It's...it's like a buzzing. A high pitched buzzing, then a whistling like a siren or something."

"Does it hurt? Is there pain?" Billie places her hands on David's ears protectively, hoping that any pain her son has will disappear with her motherly touch. But the terrifying dream she had about pulling her son's ears completely off compels her to pull her hands away.

"Just a dull ache, mostly. It's the buzzing that bothers me the most. Why won't it go away?"

"I don't know, son. I don't know."

The tinnitus in David's ears soon progresses to the point where he has problems understanding his teachers or hearing the notes on the piano the way he used to.

"Based on David's earlier symptoms - the nausea, vomiting, the vertigo - my educated guess is that David has Meniere's Disease," Dr. McMillan reports to his parents. "There is no cure but there is medication that can ease the symptoms. We can't really pinpoint why he contracted this ailment. It's still somewhat of a medical mystery, but we'll do what we can to make him comfortable."

"First meningitis, now Meniere's disease. This is heartbreaking," Billie laments. "It's so out of the blue."

"I'm really hoping this is the extent of it, but we need to be prepared that there could be some other issues or complications with his hearing that arise."

"Like what? You mean he could get worse?" Isaac is exasperated.

"There are signs of Otosclerosis," Dr. McMillan explains. "A small boney growth inside the ear canal. It's probably been growing for some time without any indication of a problem, but now it could develop into something long term. Do either of you have any deafness in your family?"

"No, not mine," Isaac says emphatically.

"I never heard about any of my family having these problems," Billie adds. "But I don't know! Oh, my God. What if he inherited this from me?"

"Sometimes there is a genetic predisposition inherited from one parent."

Billie is beside herself with guilt and screams inside. *That dream, that dream that I stole my son's ears for myself. It wasn't just a dream. It's true!* "It's my fault! It's my fault!"

"Billie!" Isaac grabs her by the shoulders. "Stop it now. Get a hold of yourself. He didn't say that."

"Now, now, Billie," the doctor tries to console her. "You can't blame yourself at all. Without knowing if you carry such a gene you cannot put all this on yourself. We're going to do everything we can to treat him. A surgery could help. But if not, there are new hearing aids that could improve his hearing. We'll look at all angles."

"He'll be fine. This is just temporary. We'll do what it takes to make him well." Isaac is resolute now, wanting to be strong, to be prepared, to do whatever it takes to help his son.

"And if nothing works?" Billie feels her heart sinking with a deep knowing that nothing will.

"One thing at a time," Dr. McMillan suggests. "But if the worst case scenario happens and he loses his hearing, there are sign language and lip reading that will give him a good quality of life."

Otosclerosis. Billie knew it was his fate. And hers. For Dorinda had told her to prepare for what was to come:

"Your boy was normal at birth but at some point he will be old enough to move into that other consciousness, and he must lose his hearing to evolve. You must help him, teach him, nurture him, make him stronger because of his deafness, so that one day he will hear what others cannot, so he will hear the voice within."

Sensorineural hearing loss coupled with conductive hearing loss is a double whammy for David. Foreground and background noises meld together, he no longer understands voices on the telephone, some sounds are excessively loud and shrill, and everything people say is a mumble.

Months turn into years with Billie teaching David sign language and lip reading until he is expert at both. Hearing aids help with hearing certain frequencies but his ability to clearly hear any note of music is forever impaired.

Medical and surgical treatments that would normally correct the problems for some strange reason do not work for David. He will always have to rely on special hearing aids to even hear nondescript vibrations.

He withstands the pain, the surgeries and the disappointment with such courage that Sally is deeply moved, becoming even more devoted to her brother. He works diligently to keep up his normal speech, but also learns to sign expertly, and teaches Sally so they can tell private little jokes to each other. They laugh that the brutish kids at school have no idea how well he can read the cruel remarks on their lips, and together they plot adolescent revenge fantasies to get even.

David's one true solace is being able to feel the pulse of music akin to the powerful rhythm of the pounding surf. And maybe, Sally insists to her parents, David really can hear things that hearing people can't.

With every day, every year mother and son share their musical gifts, they bond in a way that only two souls who share the same affinity can experience. Gladly, David executes intricate pieces by Mozart, Liszt, Beethoven and Chopin relishing his mother's pride in him. For variety, he masters the songs of Gershwin and Porter that are some of Billie's popular favorites, assisted by the constant swing of the metronome. The most beautiful music ever written that he cannot, and might not ever hear, becomes imbued in his consciousness through the patterns of notes on the page.

"Don't ever give up your music, no matter what else happens in your life, my darling. Music is your soul calling to you, and you must listen to it, always. It will not only fulfill you, it could save your life." Billie signs and speaks with emphasis while David reads her lips.

"Save my life? What to do you mean, Mom?" David cocks his head questioningly.

"I -" she hesitates, not wanting to frighten him, careful not to divulge the profound and foreboding future that awaits him. She smooths back a lock of hair from his forehead and, courageously, gently, takes his innocent sweet face in her hands. "I mean just having something so beautiful in your life, makes it worthwhile. Music doesn't just entertain, it heals. It nurtures your intellect and bridges the divide between cultures. It opens your heart and lifts you high above all mundane realities. Music is love, it is spiritual, it is what you are made of, what we are all made of in our bodies and in our souls."

"Pretty powerful stuff," David remarks.

"The most powerful."

"Even rock 'n roll?" David teases. "I can only hear the beats but it's exciting."

"Yes," Billie concedes, "pop music does cross over to speak to people world wide. But even rock and roll has its foundation in the music of the Masters. Beethoven, Mozart, Bach - they were channels for divinely inspired melodies and harmonies. Learn this music and all your music will flourish and be important, no matter what the genre is. Remember, Beethoven had the same hearing impairment you have, and he composed some of his greatest music after he went deaf."

"Yeah, but he didn't play it so well. I'm afraid I won't be able to either."

"Beethoven didn't have digital keyboards to control the volume and create orchestral sounds."

"Someday, we might even see the sounds on a screen, like pictures in full color." David predicts.

"We just might," Billie agrees. "And you just might be the one to invent it."

"Oh, mom. How could I do that?"

Hugging him close so he cannot see her lips, Billie says, "Some things, my dear boy, you'll have to figure out for yourself."

With the aid of newly-developed hearing aids, David hears some music tones with his left ear but his right ear can discern only very loud noises or speech. Now 12, David excels in school with music and computers, and with encouragement from Billie and Dorothy he also develops a penchant for metaphysics, especially crystal power.

"Crystals are filled with musical vibrations," Billie tells him. "All these elements bind you to the universe in the here and hereafter. Just ask your Aunt Dorothy."

Isaac is exasperated with Billie's affinity for the occult. "Stop teaching the boy such fairytales. Dorothy, too. It's ridiculous."

Isaac is devastated that his son is deaf. He resists learning sign language and so can execute only the most basic phrases. "What's the point," he confesses. "I know one day David will hear again. We just have to keep looking for treatments that will work."

Billie tries to comfort her husband, who she loves as much today as the day they wed, despite their differences. "We are fortunate, Isaac. We have access to the best doctors and David has many options. Other children are not so fortunate."

"Well, they will be if I can help it. Someday Mercy ships will bring medical treatment to children and families around the world who suffer from economic oppression and the ravages of war."

"You will, Isaac. It's a wonderful goal. I wish there was never any war, no battle that would make that necessary. I'm glad that David will never have to go and fight. He's safe now."

"Because he can't hear? Billie, how can you be happy about that?"

"I'm not, I'm not. I just -" Billie cringes at the possibility that she has brought his deafness upon her son as a way to keep him safe at home. She relives the horrible dream about tearing off his ears over and over, and now her son is deaf. Billie is guilt-ridden, but a tiny, secret part of her is relieved.

"Won't Fischbacher help you? With the Mercy ships, I mean."

"Not Nathan. He's a mercenary if there ever was one. No money in charity, he says."

"Well then, you'll find other backers. You're a wonderful designer, a visionary."

"One day. But first I have to create something that no one else has thought of and make everyone want it."

* * *

"Is Mom in a mood today?" David asks his father.

Isaac nods. "She's always that way when she's doing something challenging."

David and Isaac never quite know what is on Billie's mind or in her heart, why her mood shifts, as though there is some inner torment that she is always fighting. When she isn't immersed in her music or teaching David, Billie tries her best to show some domestic skills. Sewing is the one talent she aspires to that frustrates her. Isaac praises her dogged determination but dodges her every time she comes near him with a tape measure. So, it's Sally that is gifted first with a not-so-perfect yellow pinafore that the sunshiny child feels is perfect for her.

Billie diligently presses on and by the time David is to celebrate his 13th birthday she manages to design and sew a shirt for him, a sporty blue shirt with mother-of-pearl buttons and white embroidered mono-grammed initials, DN. The flaws and shortcomings of the finished shirt do not faze David.

"This is so cool," David signs, grinning with pleasure. "I'm never going to take it off. I'll wear it until every thread is frayed, until the initials fall off and the buttons turn yellow and crack."

Billie laughs heartily. "Oh, I hardly think so. But thank you for loving it. It is a bit big for you, though. I cut the pattern with room to spare."

"So, I'll grow into it. That means I can wear it longer."

Her next sewing project is a pink sheath for herself with an intricate pattern, making the task even more daunting. Unwavering, she swears, "I'll make this dress if it's the last thing I do." Little does she know it is the last dress she will ever wear.

* * *

"Billie! Wake up! What's wrong? Wake up. You're having a bad dream." It's a pronouncement that Isaac has made to his wife many times - "You're having a bad dream" - but he never knows what torments her so much. Her panic attacks have gone on far too long for them to be post-partum depression. So Isaac just holds her close believing that he can keep her from unraveling mentally by sheer force of will.

In Billie's newest nightmare she is dying, willingly giving her life to save her son. Just as she is about to know the nothingness of death Isaac awakens her. She is soaking with perspiration and seems delirious. But in the safeness of Isaac's embrace, she is soon calmed and the trembling stops. She knows how unfair it is to keep the truth from Isaac, but she can never tell him the meaning of her prescient dreams. He would never understand. He might leave her. And that would be worse than death.

"Is this what these crazy spirits are telling me? That I have to die?" she asks Dorinda when they next meet. "They say if you die in your sleep you die in real life. Will I one day go to sleep and not wake up?"

"We all die, Billie. I can't foresee how it will happen for you. But somewhere in your consciousness you know that it was meant to be."

"To die and leave my husband, my children? That makes no sense to me. I won't have it. I won't let it happen! I'm supposed to teach David some important lesson or guide him to some great achievement. How can I do that if I'm dead, for crying out loud?"

"At some point, you will have taught him all you can in this life. You'll need to move on so that he can evolve on his own."

"I understand why I'm being punished, but why does my son have to suffer so much? First he loses his hearing and now he's going to lose his mother. What does that teach him? What does that teach either of my children? Or Isaac? That I've abandoned them, that's what. Well, I won't do it. There has to be another way. I won't leave my family."

* * *

Billie plays as though it's a matter of life and death, striking the keys with power and poetry and passion, determined to chase away the demons and transform them with the awesomeness of her technique.

The more she fights it, the more she tries to slow the march of time, the more she feels impending doom. What will happen? When? Day or night? *When I'm crossing the street and a truck will hit me, or drown when I'm swimming? Maybe I'll choke on my own cooking or I'll get struck by lighting.*

She wants one more Tarot reading, to get some clue as to what kind of death is in store for her and when, but when she goes to the plaza there is no tent and no one ever remembers there ever being one. She runs from shop to shop, begging people to remember the fortune teller, the sign that said, "Tarot Card Readings by Dorinda. Truth Seekers Welcome." They shake their heads. No tent. No fortune teller.

"I can't have imagined all this. It was real, so real." Billie relives every scenario since her first reading, every card and its profound meaning for her life. She can see and hear and feel the presence of Dorinda and Nameless, their quiet elegance and power, and her deep trust in their wisdom.

But with no proof, no evidence that she ever entered the magical tent, experienced the surreal encounters with two mystical beings , she trembles at the thought that, "Maybe they're right. Maybe they never existed and it's all been an insane dream. Maybe *I* am insane."

Chapter 8

"Mr. Nickerson. I'm so sorry to have to go over these details with you at such a painful time, but I have just a few questions about the accident." The police officer leads Isaac to a comfortable chair and sits across from him.

"I understand." Still dazed, Isaac nods his head. He is a military man after all and understands that protocol must be followed.

"It was foggy, a thick marine layer," Isaac begins. "We had - my family and I - had gone to a favorite restaurant up to Lighthouse Point for dinner. On the way home I wanted to stop at my office to pick up some blueprints, so I could work on them some more. I design ships."

"So, it was foggy and you missed the exit on the freeway, is that what happened?" The officer had been briefed earlier but wanted to hear it directly from Isaac.

"Yes, I missed the exit. I guess I was going too slow and this semi was behind me. I didn't even see it in all that fog, and he hit us from behind, or so I'm told. I barely remember, it all happened so fast."

"And your car had only one air bag? On the driver's side?"

"It's an old SUV. There was one on the passenger side, but it didn't deploy. I don't know why. I don't know…" He shakes his head and runs a trembling hand through his thick dark hair.

"Was your wife wearing a seat belt?"

"Yes…no…she was adjusting it when the collision happened. I guess it wasn't fixed. Damn it Billie! I told her to leave the belt alone until I stopped. But she wouldn't listen…or didn't have time to before I -" He begins to sob, taking all the guilt onto himself.

He remembers now that David only suffered some minor injuries. It was a miracle he wasn't hurt worse. "He's deaf, you know," Isaac informs the officer. "Maybe it was a good thing he didn't hear it coming."

"I'm very sorry about your wife," Mr. Nickerson. "But I'm glad your boy will be okay."

"Thank you." A light goes on in Isaac's head. "Oh, my God. Sally. My daughter. I've got to go see her. She's in the ICU. She might not wake up."

"Of course. I think we're finished here. If there is anything I can do for you, don't hesitate to call." He gives Isaac his card.

But now Isaac and David must concentrate on Sally. Glumly, they walk together to the ICU and to Sally's room. They are surprised to see her awake.

"She's still groggy," the doctor explains, "and not quite sure where she is."

"Sally," Isaac soothes her. "It's Dad and David. We're here for you."

"Where am I, Dad? What's going on?"

"You're in the hospital, Sally. There was an accident. You got pretty banged up."

"I did? Were you hurt? And David?"

"We were very lucky, Sal," David tells her with a quick sign. "We'll both be good as new soon."

"Mom…was Mom hurt?"

Deliberately avoiding the question, Isaac focuses on his daughter's condition. He forces an encouraging smile.

"Right now, we've got to get you better." Isaac turns to the doctor for an update.

"I was just going to give her a check up," the doctor informs him. "Her vitals are good and that's a good sign. Sally, I need to examine your mobility now. Okay?"

"Okay, I guess." Sally says meekly.

"Now hold your right hand up to mine and push back as hard as you can. Good. Nice and strong. Same with your left hand. That's fine, too. Do this with your fingers." The doctor touches his thumb to each finger and Sally mirrors his movements.

"You're doing fine, Sally. Now, we'll check your feet and legs, okay?"

"Sure."

The doctor lifts the sheet above Sally's knees. "Can you wiggle your toes for me?"

"Sure. Is that okay?"

There is no movement, but Sally doesn't realize it. "Try again, Sally," Isaac encourages her. You can do it."

Still no movement. The doctor runs a small blunt instrument along the soles of Sally's feet. There is no reflex motion.

"What's going on, Doc? Why can't she move her legs?" Isaac is borderline panicky. "Can't you do something?"

"We'll have to do more tests to be sure. When she came in we did a CT scan but couldn't see anything to indicate paralysis."

"But she can't move her legs?" Isaac tried not to sound hysterical.

Sally starts to sob. "I can't move, David. I can't move my legs!"

Her brother holds Sally's hand and signs to her, "It's okay, Sal. You're going to be okay. I promise."

An MRI to detect fractures or nerve damage to Sally's spine is performed but doesn't yield any definitive diagnosis.

"She does have some compression fractures and tissue swelling," the Radiologist reports, "so we hope these will heal on their own. But whether or not she will regain all of her functionality is too soon to tell. We are hopeful the paralysis is temporary."

"And if it isn't?" Isaac's breathing is heavy with anxiety.

"Let's take it one step at a time."

Outside Sally's room, Dorothy tries to console Isaac to face the most difficult undertaking of his life.

"I don't think I can tell Sally about her mother without completely falling apart," Isaac confesses. "Finding out she can't walk is bad enough, but telling her that Billie is dead will devastate her."

"It's devastated all of us," Dorothy reminds him, "but we'll all be by her side when you tell her. You have to do it soon, Isaac. This is not something you can keep from her much longer."

"One day she's all happy and carefree, then in an instant she's motherless and an invalid. It's not fair." Isaac finally breaks down, his body heaving in sorrowful cries.

* * *

David guides his sister's wheelchair up to Billie's casket where they will see their mother for the last time. Wearing the pink sheath that she had designed and sewn herself, with her luxurious hair a cascade of silken blonde waves, Billie Nickerson is beautiful even in death. David steels himself to keep composed, for Sally's sake.

"She looks like she's sleeping, David," Sally remarks. "Sleeping Beauty. Maybe she'll wake up. Wake up, Mom." She grabs onto the edge of the coffin and lays her head in her hands, crying her heart out.

David puts his arms around his sister's shoulders and comforts her tenderly. Throughout the funeral service he is stunned but stoic, relieved that he cannot hear the platitudes of well-meaning friends or the sobs of the sister he adores.

Isaac is so despondent that Dorothy has to be the strong one, to keep her brother from letting his knees buckle under him.

Billie is laid to rest in the Nickerson family cemetery overlooking the ocean, which today is smooth as glass, gilded by the sun's sparkling gold reflection.

An alabaster guardian angel adorns her headstone which reads,

Blanche "Billie" Nickerson
Beloved Wife and Mother
We Miss You

David, Sally, Isaac and Dorothy place single stem yellow roses on her coffin one by one and say their goodbyes, their pain assuaged by the fact that she is close by and they can visit her anytime they feel the need.

Even in her spirit state, Billie feels their sorrow and makes a solemn vow of her own. *I'm coming back, dear family. I don't know when or how, but I promise I won't desert you."*

Chapter 9

In the Time Between Time

Billie scans the staging area. The auditorium is filled to capacity with people milling about in their seats with anticipation. Only they are not human entities, they are spirits of various levels of experience denoted by their auric colors, ranging from shades of white to yellow to blue.

The orchestra pit is vibrant with violet energies, demonstrating through music the highest form of spiritual evolution. Every instrument is represented, from ancient celestas, lyres and lutes to zithers, keyboards and horns of every type.

Billie is astonished. "What is this place? Some sort of performing hall? I never imagined that heaven - or wherever I am - would look like this."

"This was your life experience, Billie. The concert hall, the musicians, the crowds. Your spirit experience will mirror your earthly experience, until you are ready to let go of it."

"Why are there so many different colors of people?"

"That's where they are in their soul evolution, each one having achieved a higher state of development through their music experience."

"But why do I have no color at all? I think I'm pretty highly developed musically."

"Because you've just begun. You are white, Blanche, a shining light but a very young soul."

"That's odd. I've always felt like an old soul."

"A popular New Age expression."

Billie appreciates her guide's humor, and a feeling of familiarity comes through. "I know you, don't I? I've seen you before. Why, you're that fortune teller from the tent. Not Dorinda, but the other one. I never knew your name."

"Names are not important here. I was on a mission that required me to have no identity."

"A mission? For me?"

"You didn't think you were just there in that tent having a Tarot card reading, did you?"

"Obviously not. But you, and Dorinda - you never really existed. You were just a figment. No one ever saw you but me, never even saw that tent or the sign inviting people in for readings."

"As it was meant to be."

Billie moves freely through this first experience, then on through various portals. People that she recognizes from her Earth life are formless, ethereal energies: an aunt from her father's side of the family who passed on just before Billie moved to Port Avalon; a cousin who was killed in a plane crash during his first solo flight; a friend from high school who succumbed to leukemia; a teacher who committed suicide when his wife left and took their children with her. Their faceless forms nod in recognition as they move along on their own personal missions.

Then, emerging through a diaphanous curtain, two figures appear to Billie. They are old now, their auras grayed by their harsh life experiences. Billie had seen them rarely in her last years on Earth, living miles apart as they did, then finally parted by tragedy and death. But now, as they stand face to face, all the hurt, the anger, the conflicts they engaged in, the feelings of lonely isolation they instilled in her, the insecurities and unworthiness they passed on to her...all those feelings come to the fore and she feels on edge, a tenseness even in this sweet afterlife dimension.

If I hadn't left them, if I had stayed near them, they would still be alive. Maybe I could have saved them from that burning building, from an arsonist's senseless evil.

But then they embrace, and in their need for her, in their longing, Billie senses their sad regret, the apologies they can't express, the forgiveness they offer her. She melts into their agony and it transforms into her love for them. Dissolving into a violet light, they are at last free souls.

"This is more than I can bear!" Billie cries. "I thought there was no pain or heartache here. Why do I remember them, my mother and father, and all the turmoil we went through?"

"Your eternal identity never leaves you," Nameless tells her. "In time you will experience a cloud of amnesia, feel less emotion, where you choose to remember nothing of the past."

"Choose? You mean I have choices here?"

"We are coming to the choice arena now," Nameless informs her. "The newly dead - I don't like to use that word because I don't consider you dead. You are very much alive here, but mortals have chosen to use such a label. Moving on - this is where you realize that everything in your life - every experience and encounter - was something you chose to do before you were even consciously aware."

"You mean before I was born?"

"Sometimes it's a pre-life choice, sometimes it is an unconscious realization immediately after birth."

"God, I made so many bad choices…"

"And so many good ones, Billie."

"Like dying in a car crash?"

"That, too."

"My son hates me for that choice. How do I fix that?"

"You're not here to fix the past, but to decide where you will go in the future."

"You mean Reincarnation?"

"That's one option."

"There are others?"

"I don't usually let my students know that they have choices, unless I think they need to know."

"But we do! We do. What if I choose to go back to my family?"

"You know that's not possible."

"But sometimes spirits do connect with their loved ones. I've seen Mediums help them do that."

"What I'm saying is that you cannot physically return as the same person in the same point in time. You cannot communicate with your family unless they summon you."

Billie is crestfallen. Her son hates her, wants nothing to do with her. He wouldn't summon her in a million years.

"I have to find a way. I have to make them understand."

"If it's meant to be you will make your spirit felt by them. But you have a lot of lessons to learn first. It will take a long time."

"I don't have time!"

"Billie, dear, you have nothing *but* time. You have an eternity."

Billie wants to grab Nameless by the shoulders and shake her, but there is nothing to grab, nothing to hold on to. "Help me, please. You have to help me reach them somehow, some way. My children don't have an eternity. My son is deaf…"

"His choice to hear the music you have imbued in his soul."

"My daughter may never walk again…"

"She has chosen to have her brother care for her and she has someone to worship now that you are gone."

"And Isaac - he is lost, so lost. He might never recover."

"He will find his way back, in time"

"My husband is not like me or you. He doesn't believe in the supernatural. I don't think he believes in anything at this point."

Against the rules and against her better judgment, Billie's guide confides, "There is another place where you can reside and work things through. Come."

Billie follows closely as they move across a threshold of soft light and mist where she is awed by a vision that is stunning in its realism.

"What is this?"

"Here, you will see through a window of sorts all that is happening with your family. Everything they do or think or experience you will witness. It will frustrate you not to be able to connect with them or let them know you are with them."

"So, it's my punishment, for the things I've done or contemplated doing for selfish reasons."

"We don't punish here. And certainly not just for thoughts. If we did, we'd never have time for anything else. You are here to learn, to understand what on Earth are called mistakes, and to move on to higher love."

"But what is the point of just watching and wanting?"

"You won't just be watching. Concurrently, you will have to move on to other times and places. You may have to repeat things over and over. You will be close enough to touch your boy, but will not be able to physically do it. One day, if your son desires to communicate with you, you will be there in spirit."

"But how will he know? How will I know I've broken through?"

"He will feel you. It might be a light brush stroke on his arm or a breath of air on his face, but he will know you are there."

"And my other choice?"

"You can go to the Other Side, the blissful hereafter where you completely let go of your memories of human life and move on to your eternal paradise."

This latter choice, Billie decides, is no choice at all. Somehow, someway she will break through that wall that separates their realities, penetrate that window of time, and return to her family before it's too late.

Chapter 10

Nameless leaves Billie alone to do a "chore." This surprises Billie for she never knew there were chores in wherever this is after you die. She learns, however, that spirits in the hereafter are quite busy working, learning, creating in all manner of activities. Certainly not the same as they did in their mortal life, but more in thought, visualization and telepathic conversation.

"It's not like you thought it would be, is it?"

Billie feels a presence by her side that makes her uncomfortable. "Who are you? What do you want?"

"I am your Dark Side, Billie."

A rush of chilling air, an ethereal gasp of fright, rips through Billie at this admonition. That's what the sinister dark cloud had said to her while it hovered creepily on her keyboard one afternoon while she played Chopin's Nocturne, rendering it into discord.

"You again! What are you? How are you here? You don't belong."

"No, I don't belong here. So I escape now and then from the limbo that enslaves me and find my way back to that lively, exciting realm of Earth. Oh, how I love to taunt human beings like you, so pretentious and self-absorbed."

"I'm not! I mean, I wasn't. Who are you to judge? How dare you say that to me?"

That familiar mean-spirited laughter echoes through the boundless ether, changing Billie's soft blue cocoon to a dusky shroud.

"I dare because you need to know there is more here in this infinity than the monotony and exasperation of The Watching Place and the fantastical, unreachable Other Side. Looking through that Window of Time is fruitless. It's the real purgatory that people on Earth talk about when they believe punishment awaits them after they die. Don't let your foolish spirit guide deceive you and pretend otherwise."

"She's not foolish. And why would she deceive me? What has she to gain?"

"It's a game played here by so-called superior souls who want you to be helpless and powerless."

"I don't believe you. Get away from me."

"All right, I'll go - if you are fine with never reaching your precious son or seeing your family again. But what if I told you," the Dark Side suggests conspiratorially, "there is a way you can have all that you desire?"

"What - what do you mean?"

"What if I told you," the hooded, faceless entity taunts Billie, "that you could reincarnate as anyone, any time you wished?"

"No, that's not possible. I can't choose when and whom."

"Don't believe that drivel. Come with me and I'll show you how it's done."

As though mesmerized Billie follows. They stop at the front of a vast entrance, an indescribable barrier with no form or substance. What lies beyond she cannot see, but the Dark Side lures her on with a carrot dangling at the end of a stick: she will be with her family again, and with her son, to finish what she began as his mother.

"On the other side of this entry is the key to your dilemma, the vehicle to escaping this prison of your own making, the means to rid yourself of your guilt and be free to return to your former life. Just step over the portal and you'll see."

"I can't. I can't see past it."

"You mean you don't want to see it. Get over yourself or you're never going to move on."

With the determination that served her well in life, Billie consents, and steps into the abyss. Shockingly, however, what she sees is completely contrary to what the Dark Side implies. This is no trouble free environ with spirits floating on the breeze of carelessness. Instead, it is an endless sea of souls lost in the dull, quiet chaos of deep despair. They never speak to each other, just shuffle aimlessly along, heads down, with lifeless eyes.

The weight of their past transgressions is profound and they carry it like millstones. They all but have a letter "G" branded on their foreheads, reminding them of the guilt they carry and don't know how to shed.

Terrified, Billie backs out, returning to safety. "I can't go there. I am not like them." Billie struggles with her conscience. "I'm not. Am I?"

Dark Side tells her she is not so pure, for she lied to Isaac about her affair, about her psychic experiences, about her dreams of taking her son's - *his* son's - hearing so he would never be a soldier at war.

"But I did that to protect him," Billie protests, "to protect both of them from suffering."

"And what about your sister? The one you encouraged to join in a peace protest that cost her life?"

"I didn't - I mean, it was what she wanted to do. How could I know how it would turn out?"

"What about her suffering? Do you want to carry that memory with you for eternity?"

"No. No, I don't," she whispers.

"Then go through the portal and linger for but a moment, reliving your torment. Take your punishment, then be done with it forever. Only then can you burst free of your lifeless shroud to be with your loved ones again."

The remorse is more than Billie can bear and she yields to the belief that some penalty is warranted. Determined to make any atonement to return to her family Billie makes the decision to feel that quickening of sacrifice, that momentary agony that will cleanse her sins. But just as she is about to cross the threshold, a warning clarion resounds, freezing her spirit in midair.

"Not one more step! Or it will be your last, Billie Nickerson! There is no returning from The Left Door," Nameless cautions, swiftly returning to Billie's side.

"But if I can see my family again…"

"Never. Not there. The Dark Side lies. Its wicked nature is to render needless punishment. You must trust what I tell you."

"I - I don't know. Dark Side warned me that you were not being truthful with me."

"This is how evil works. Whether it's inside of you as your dark side or in the mortal world, you must fight it any way that you can."

"Who do I believe? *What* do I believe?" she implores.

"Believe in love, Billie. Believe in those who love you, have always loved you, and will always love you."

"Isaac did. Sally did. David did, once. And now he hates me."

"Who prayed for you when you lay dying on that gurney? Who would have changed places with you as the breath left your body? Who would give anything to have you at peace and at rest?"

Billie's tears flow like pearls and find their way to the burdened hearts of her daughter, her husband, and her son. "They would," she knows down deep. "They would."

Chapter 11

Moving with the speed of angels who are not tethered to the restrictions of time and space, Nameless arrives at the Hall of Justice to stand before the Elders and beseech them to intervene in Billie Nickerson's Life Chart.

"She must not enter the Holding Place where her Dark Side taunts her with human guilt feelings. I thought she would be strong enough to resist, or that my guidance would be enough for her to choose the light of the Other Side. But she wavers. Apparently I have failed."

"There is no failure upon you," one of the Elders says. "As with all souls Billie Nickerson has the freedom to choose which path she will take, even in the hereafter, even if it means succumbing to the evil that would destroy her."

"But please, look at her Chart. It is imperative that she choose rightly, for it has been written that she is to inspire her son to heroic achievements."

"It looks as though she has taught him well. She has been an inspiration. Now he is on his own."

"But," Nameless insists, "Billie fights this notion. She still holds to some of her earthly sentiments. That her son declared he would hate her if she died has put an enormous burden on her soul. She is tormented with misgivings about her purpose from here on."

"What is your wish?" the Elder inquires.

"For an emergency intervention. Show the love and compassion, the wisdom for which you are revered."

The Elders deliberate the situation quietly, dispassionately, for theirs in not a governing body. They make no laws or decrees, and they rarely interfere in a soul's journey.

"We have decided, in Billie Nickerson's best interests, to have her appear before us and make her case. It seems she has died before her time. She was not meant to be here so soon."

"A mistake?" Nameless has known this to happen, but wonders how she could have missed it. She is admired for her careful attention to the most minute detail when a soul is on the brink of death. "Then it would be merciful to intervene. She must be shown a way to be at peace with her premature decision to die."

"We are not so sure it was her own decision."

Nameless is shocked to hear this. How could someone else interfere with Billie's fate? What kind of influence would this other being have over her to make her die before her time?

Nameless ruminates over the circumstances of Billie's impending demise following her accident, and the scenario looms large as surgeons work feverishly to repair a ruptured blood vessel next to Billie's heart…

"She's going down!"

Don't fight it Billie. I am here with you. Just let go."

"Stop compressions… Check pulse…" There is none.

That's it, dear. Just a few more seconds now and we can walk your path together.

"Charge paddles to 300… Clear!" Repeated electric shocks fail to revive Billie and she flatlines. Reluctantly, the doctors accept they can do no more to save her life.

"Want to call it?"

"Time of death 17:40."

"Wait, wait!" The pulse on the monitor is weak but measurable. One doctor checks her eye response while the other checks Billie's respiration.

"No response in the pupils. No brain activity."

"No breath sounds."

"Yet the monitor shows a pulse." The doctor places his stethoscope on Billie's chest. "It's erratic and faint. It's not possible. But let's intubate and maybe..."

Don't hesitate, Billie. Your time on this earth is done.

No. Wait. I'm afraid. I don't want to leave yet.

I know. But remember this is what you wanted. And it's my task to make your transition easy, to take you where you are meant to reside for eternity...

Nameless is devastated. As Billie's guide it was she who coaxed her to let go of her mortality. Billie didn't want to leave. In that moment she had changed her mind, but Nameless was unwavering in her belief that this was Billie's time to die.

She recalled how Billie's son David was angry and distraught that his mother did not try harder to live.

"Mom," he had whispered. "I know you're in there. I know you can hear me. Come back to us. Just try harder. I know you can do it. You taught me everything I know - music, sign language - you taught me to never give up no matter what. Please, please. Don't give up now."

He grabbed his mother's hand desperately.

"No! Mom, if you die I'll hate you forever! I'll never forgive you for leaving me!"

You didn't tell me he would hate me! Please bring me back so I can explain!

It's too late, Billie. We can't bring you back. This was the deal. Your life for David's soul, for his gifts to the world.

"It's too late," Nameless had said. It was *she*, Billie's guide, the one spirit who was to act in Billie's best interest in life and in the afterlife, who had taken the decision to live or die out of her hands.

The Elders now understand, but without judgement on Nameless who will render judgement upon herself.

"Billie's Chart also has delineated that she has many lessons to learn in many other lifetimes before she can be ready to inspire the heart of her son again."

"And as for my role?" Nameless asks, intuitively knowing the answer. "I will step aside. She will be in your charge from this moment on."

Hearing the news that it was a mistake for her to die so soon, Billie implores the Council to allow her to go back, even if it is in a different body as someone her family doesn't know. Just for the chance to correct her mistakes and guide her son's path.

"There are many life lessons that must be cleared away first," she is told. "This is the only way to correct your mistakes."

"How long? How many lifetimes?"

"Time does not exist to a spirit soul. Past, Present and Future are all one dimension," the Elder reminds her. "When you learn this, your other incarnations will pass in a blink. Resist, and the moments will expand into eons."

"I don't know any other life but my own. I wouldn't know how to act, what to believe or what to do."

"Well, that *is* the point, is it not?" The Elders laugh not cruelly but at the irony that all newly-deceased fall prey to.

Willing to bear uncertainty, pain and agony in lives not of her choosing or liking, but believing the experiences will bring her closer to her son, Billie resigns herself to an unknown number of reincarnations.

Chapter 12

"Run, Little One, run as fast as you can!"

The vicious whooping and hollering are close on the child's heels as she and her mother make a breathless attempt to escape. The marauding band of Mongol renegades tear through the village, setting fire to every house, beheading the men, torturing the women, and taking children hostage.

Little One and her Mother are fast on their feet as they sprint out of sight of their predators. With bare feet bleeding, they take refuge in a deserted hut and gasp for air trying to catch their breath.

"I can't go anymore, Mama," Little One cries. Mother wraps her strong arms around the child and promises to protect her. "We'll rest here for awhile. They won't find us now."

Fatigued beyond their ability to stay alert, they both fall asleep and dream peaceful dreams of being safe and warm in a new home in a new village.

Soon, their breathing becomes heavy, their chests tight and unyielding. Even in a deep sleep they sense the air is unbreathable and something is choking their lives away. Mother and Little One awaken just as inescapable flames engulf them and suffocating smoke blackens their lungs.

Returning to earth, leaving the sanctuary of the afterlife world and the lightness of being to fall back into the heavy burdensome body of mortality, is the hardest decision for a spirit soul to make. As a beginner soul, Billie's first reincarnations manifest in diverse, unconnected life cycles. She is man, woman, mother, father, sibling, with lives as mundane or as sensational as one can imagine. She lives long, or dies young, or meets with violent ends.

Billie is exasperated by her own inability to choose a productive and meaningful life. Is she the victim of her own internal discord, she wonders? Are these cruel cosmic jokes or the irony of her own misguided choices? Does she sense some need to punish herself by attracting horrible life experiences? *Is it because I left my parents alone to pursue my own dreams? If I had stayed would they still be alive? Could I have saved them from that burning building?*

She recalls the miscarriages that she had, the little souls whose lives were ended before they even began. *Did they change their minds about being born to me because I was not worthy of them, or because they had a better life waiting for them with another mother? Or did they decide to die, wisely knowing that they had to make way for David to be born?*

"Can I ever know even one serene life? One existence that is the stepping stone to my true desire?" Billie rails to the Council. "It has to be my compensation for all this agony. Otherwise what is the point?"

"Life and death," the Elders explain to her, "are mere pieces of a puzzle, with each life a touchstone and a link to the next and the next, and ultimately to the last. How spirits learn to assemble them, to create the basic design of their diverse lives, determines if they can move to a higher level of soul evolution. And so it is with you, Billie, how ingenious can you be in creating your life experiences?"

How ingenious, really! Occupying the beleaguered lives of people on Earth to whom she has no relationship is antithetical to her true goal. Life does not seem to be kind to women young or old, in Billie's karmic life chain, nor is it any better as a man. Karma is gender neutral, rendering harsh lessons equally. But none of these experiences stick or fulfill her mission, or make any significant mark, and so they are forgotten and blown away like whispers in the wind.

Exhausted by her seemingly endless stream of embodiments, and hoping that she soon will clear away her karmic obligations, Billie stands before the Window of Time, watching her loved ones go on without her. She is close enough to touch them but still there is that vexing dimensional separation.

If she had a human heart, she would feel it pound and flutter with eagerness every time she saw them. There would also be the aching that comes with feeling sad and anguished by what they have to endure without her. But even without a human heart Billie knows deep in her soul that their lives are still intertwined with hers, that their bond is timeless and without end.

And so she perseveres.

As long as she does not give in to the required "crossing over" that is the lot of the dead, as long as she holds onto the conviction that she can somehow influence their lives, she knows that she will be with her family again.

To make the waiting bearable in this beautiful space of time between time, Billie turns to the one passion that liberated her from all of mortal life's disappointments, troubles and sadness. The one thing that lifted her heart and allied her to life's meaning, to her son: music, glorious and divine music, the music she was gifted with and, in turn, gifted to David.

As she creates and performs, filling the ether with harmonies that soothe and levitate, she can feel her son's presence and he can feel hers, as though they are playing a duet inspired by the memory of the other.

She caresses the piano keys with love and an artist's skill, hears the melodies and chords flow easily from her fingers, allows herself to be a channel for the enduring music created by inspired masters. With every note she also watches and contemplates, fantasizing her escape from the afterlife.

Chapter 13

David and Sally Nickerson love their father but he has become so distant and guilt-ridden in these months following Billie's death that he cannot connect to his children they way he once did. Isaac is especially disdainful of David's affinity for crystals and the occult that his sister Dorothy encourages by bringing new magic "rocks" to him after each of her excursions abroad. This was also Billie's doing and her undoing. Her obsessive belief in the paranormal kept driving them further apart. He couldn't compete with it or even understand it.

Isaac so bitterly regrets that his daughter is bound to a wheelchair from the accident he caused that he is blind to her buoyant spirit and the light in her eyes. Or perhaps he resents that the light in those eyes is for David only, the brother she worships. As her father, he determines to raise the money for the operation that could help her walk again, but deep inside he is terrified that the operation could also kill her.

"I'll give you a share of my royalties for the new ship designs, Nathan. It's the only way I could pay you back."

"If they're that good, Isaac, why not give them to me outright and I'll finance your daughter's medical bills?"

"I can't do that, Nathan," Isaac declines. "I'm an independent contractor and the designs belong to me."

"We might just have to fight that out in court," Nathan subtly threatens.

"For Pete's sake, Nathan, can't you be just be human about this and help a little girl walk again?"

"That would be sentimental on my part, something I can't afford to mix with business."

Billie paces back and forth wishing she could grab Nathan Fischbacher by the throat and squeeze the life from him. How dare he disrespect Isaac's brilliance or refuse to advance Isaac the money for Sally's operation.

She pounds on the Window with her fists but there is no sound except a dull echo. No shouts or screams penetrate that invincible separation between Billie and Isaac. Into the void she vows, "You will pay for this Nathan! By God I will make you pay!"

Nameless is beside herself. Knowing she cannot intervene directly, or appeal to the Elders, she beseeches Dorinda to help.

"It's my fault, Dorinda. I failed to guide her properly and she died too soon. I don't understand how I could have done such a disastrous thing."

"This is no time for recriminations," Dorinda consoles her friend.

"But she is so desperate to break through I fear Billie will do something so counter to her highest good that it will destroy her."

"I will come up with a plan that will set things right," Dorinda promises. "The primary goal has always been to lead David to his destiny, so I have to find a way to help him achieve that goal."

"We may be running out of time. If Billie can't reach him, how will that happen? Will he know what to do?"

"I have to take it up with the highest, wisest and most authoritative of the Elders."

"You mean the Other?"

"Exactly."

Dorinda's soul is of the most advanced level. She has paid her karmic debts, has been a beloved and revered Spirit Guide through a millennia of lifetimes. But never has she stood on the precipice of such an important moment in time and she is unsure how to proceed.

"I have never made such a request of you, never imagined I would even entertain such a request. But I would be willing to give up my spiritual post in order to become earthbound once again, so that I may help right a wrong - the premature death of Billie Nickerson - so that I may help to guide her son to his calling."

"This is highly unusual," the Other remarks. "No spirit at your level of enlightenment has had this selfless aspiration. Why is it so important to you?"

"It is important to the world. His mother is not evolved enough to contact her son, and I fear that time is running out. There are happenings in the world that David must set right, but he needs inspiration and guidance. And a bit of a spiritual nudge."

"And you believe you can achieve this?"

"I do. I foresee the direction that David must follow, and can help connect him to the right experiences."

"If you believe in this quest, Dorinda, I believe in you. I will grant your wish to become earthbound again. But know that I will always be by your side, for your challenges will be many and the will of a mere mortal will not be enough to meet them. You will retain some of your spiritual powers, for you will need them to succeed."

"I am grateful. I will not fail you."

Before Dorinda is excused, the Other posits a question: "What of Billie Nickerson? What of her longing to return to her old life? Will your stepping up to help her son assuage her? Keep her from trying?"

Dorinda pauses, but only briefly. With a smile she replies, "Knowing Billie, she will never give up. She is a challenge, and You and the Elders will have to be most creative in your dealings with her."

Chapter 14

As David mourns the loss of his mother, bears the sad weight of his sister's paralysis, and feels powerless to help his father deal with crushing guilt, his music becomes secondary in his life. It reminds him too much of what he lost when his mother died. She took with her the love of music that she game him. Touching the keys is too painful, not hearing the music is more agonizing than challenging.

Instead he finds solace in working with the collection of crystals his mother and his aunt gave him. They represent a power he can see and feel, one that he is determined to understand and master.

It is a beautiful summer afternoon when David kneels on the sand, removes the gems from a pouch he carries and begins to arrange them in a circle.

Sally maneuvers her wheelchair along the private pier from the house and down a specially built ramp that allows her to come down to the beach next to him.

David looks up to see her. "Hi, Sally. I didn't know you were there."

"What are you doing with your crystals?" Sally signs as deftly as David does, and their conversations alternate between signing and lip reading.

"I just gave them a good overnight cleansing in the salt water and I want them to sit out in the sun awhile."

"Why are you doing that?"

"I've been working with them a lot lately and they need to be reenergized," David explains. "A good electrical storm would also help to make them strong again, and I could study their individual molecular structure and vibrational patterns better, but there doesn't seem to be much chance of that today."

Sally shares David's fascination with the "magic rocks," more out of adoration for her older brother than an affinity for the crystals themselves. But it helps that he is able to bring some laughter and enjoyment to Sally as he entertains her with his made-up stories about each crystal's significance.

"Tell me about them again, David, where they came from and what their powers are."

"Okay." David knows Sally prefers the mystical legends to all that science stuff about atoms, neutrons, and protons. So he plays these sessions with his sister up to the hilt by giving her the most imaginative descriptions he can conjure up.

He holds up a deep violet-colored quartz crystal. "This one is an amethyst," David begins. "It was used in ancient cultures as an amulet to prevent drunkenness. The people got stoned instead."

Sally's blonde ponytail bobs perkily when she throws her head back and laughs.

One by one David picks up a brilliant colored stone and weaves a silly and fantastic tale, delighting Sally with every word.

"Show me the pretty pink one. It's my favorite."

"It's beautiful, isn't it." David holds a deep rose-colored crystal. "It works on the frequency of faith and unconditional love." He signs the word love, and gives the crystal to Sally to hold. "I'm going to have this set in a pendant for you to wear next to your heart. That's where it really belongs."

Sally's eyes mist over and she, too, signs as she whispers, "Oh, David, I love you, too." But when she sees the Singer, she squeals with delight. "David! Let me see that one."

David holds up the Singer, a unique boat-shaped white quartz crystal, so she can see it from every angle. "Isn't it excellent?"

Sally is almost breathless. "It looks just like a sailing ship! I've never seen anything like it!"

"There isn't another like it in the whole world," David boasts. "I call it my Crystal Clipper," he says and signs, "a ship to take me to far off, magical places – with the help of my imagination, of course."

"Oh, David, wouldn't it be wonderful if you could sail off to a magical place where all your dreams could come true?"

"And if I did, I'd take you with me, Sal, to a place where you would walk and dance and be happy again." He spins her wheelchair a few turns.

"And where you could hear again," Sally adds, as though the dream just might be possible. "So, if we're going to sail off on a Crystal Clipper, hadn't you better get your magic rocks all re-energized? It looks like it's going to rain any minute."

David looks up, surprised to see that dark clouds are beginning to appear. "Aye, Captain. You're right. This might be a good time to try that new energy formation I just read about."

It soothes Billie as she watches brother and sister bond together with love and admiration. But when David begins to experiment with a powerful crystal grid Billie tries frantically to warn him not to play around with something he knows nothing about. Of course he cannot hear her and Billie is beside herself with worry.

David picks up a small twig and draws a pyramid shape in the sand. Then he draws an inverted pyramid over the other pattern, creating a six-pointed Star of David.

Sally crinkles her nose. "What's an energy formation?"

"They're really called gridwork patterns. I don't know much about them yet, but this double pyramid is supposed to be very powerful for something. I'll have to read up on it more."

"David, do you think you should experiment with it yet? Something awful could happen."

But David is oblivious to her concern. Already he is placing a crystal strategically on each point of the star, with the sparkling Singer at the apex of the pyramid.

Just as he completes the grid pattern, a crackling bolt of lightning streaks across the sky, skitters along the surface of the water, and strikes the Singer full on. Acting as a conduit of energy, the Singer transmits the lightning to every crystal in the grid, emblazoning the sand in a kaleidoscopic fury. The force throws David over on his back and knocks him out cold.

Billie is seized with fear. But worse, when she realizes Sally has completely disappeared from her wheel chair Billie's fright turns to terror. She screams for David to wake up, for someone to help him.

"Let me out!" Billie cries, futilely pounding on the window but not making a sound. "Let me help him! We have to find my daughter!"

A sudden overwhelming force whisks her away from the Window of Time, keeping her from knowing what has happened to her children.

"You have not yet earned the right to intervene."

"What do I have to do? I don't understand. How can I earn the right?"

In a shadowy tunnel, devoid of light or hope, a gloomy spirit hovers around Billie, a bitter and angry soul she feels a familiarity with but can't quite recognize.

"I want you to leave here, Billie, but not as some savior saint. Go back to Earth and suffer the loss of your children and your husband."

"How dare you! Why do you want to torment me? I don't even know you."

"Yes you do. I tried to warn you a couple of times but you didn't listen. Not when I appeared in your room before your wedding, not when I danced on your piano and delighted in almost scaring the life out of you."

"That was you?"

"Yes. One and the same, who also offered you an opportunity to reincarnate through the Holding Place portal but you were too chicken to take the risk."

"They warned me about *you*. That's why I changed my mind."

"They warned you and what did it get you? Nothing. Just more frustration standing in front of that stupid Window of Time, unable to touch your family, your beloved son."

"What could you have done! Why should I trust you?"

"Because now I want you to go back, go back as someone they don't know and don't want to know."

"But, why? What's in it for you?"

"Just as your son hates you for dying, I will never forgive you for wishing me dead."

"What are you talking about? Who are - oh, my God." As the veil of obscurity lifts, Billie sees the entity before her. The hollow orbs transform into penetrating blue eyes, her aura changes from murky brown to a soft blue. Billie knows at once who she is. "It's you."

"Yes, Billie. It's me. Long gone and forgotten."

"Forgotten? Never. But what are you talking about. I never wished you dead. How can you say such a thing? You are my older sister and I love you - I always loved you."

"You encouraged me to risk my life by joining in that senseless campus protest. Remember?"

"I did not. You went willingly. Don't *you* remember?"

"No. It was your staunch pacifist ideology that convinced me, Billie."

"Don't blame me for your decision. I was so young and idealistic, but you were always so pigheaded. No one could have swayed you, not even me."

"You practically brainwashed me with your pontificating. I can see from your sad life that you never changed."

"I don't understand what you are thinking now, Fallon. I admired you. I was inspired by your courage. How could I have known that violence would erupt, that some trigger-happy guard would open fire on a bunch of college students demonstrating against war?"

Billie takes a long breath, summoning up some compassion. "Fallon, my dear sister, I'm so sorry you died. But by now you should have crossed over to find some peace. Instead you hang around like a tortured ghost. What good is that?"

"I could ask you the same question, Billie. What makes you think you are so special that you can go back to Earth and guide your son to some sort of Messianic destiny?"

"I - I was told that it was my mission. Because *David* is special, not me. He has the gifts that can make the world a better place."

"Well, just leave him alone to do that. Don't go back just to muck things up for him."

"I *have* to go back, Fallon. I died too soon."

Fallon laughs hysterically. "*You* died too soon? Well now that makes me feel better. Vengeance is no longer mine. The Fates have done it for me."

"You don't understand. My absence is causing David such heartache that he can't see what is in front of him. It's causing him to make disastrous mistakes."

"Blinded by his hatred for you, for choosing to die when you just might have lived if you made the right choices."

"No, no, it was a mistake. My guide made a mistake. She didn't listen to me. I had changed my mind at the last minute. Even the doctors felt it, the faint heartbeat, my effort to stay alive."

"Oh, please, Billie. It isn't your Nameless guide who is to blame, it's you, for not having your seat belt on. Something so basic and simple could have saved your life!"

"That doesn't matter now. All that matters is my family, my son. He is confused about what he must do and why he was chosen to do it. Please, don't be angry with me, Fallon. Help me. As your sister. If you know a way back, please help me."

"Yes, I'll help you, Billie. But you might wish I didn't."

Chapter 15

One Last Reincarnation

As Billie hurtles downward from the beyond, life experiences flash by. Holographic images dance before her encased in Dorinda's crystal ball: a glistening, ghostlike ship that she doesn't recognize appears out of the mist; the sound of sweet music delights the air but it's a song she has never heard.

There are Isaac, Sally and David at her graveside laying flowers next to her tombstone. Frantically Billie wills the petals to spin in the air, to dance with joyous abandon, then settle down as still as the grave-yard's spirits. Her heart as heavy as it could ever have been in mortal life, Billie mourns her ineffectiveness when her family leaves without acknowledging the sign.

Dear family, didn't you know it was me trying to reach you. Didn't you feel my spirit in the fluttering blossoms, my touch in the breeze?

Bizarrely now, she hovers three feet above reality, the real world where her family resides. The topography she walks is a mirror image of theirs but it is as pure a landscape as one can imagine, a reflection of the earth from thousands of years ago when bodies of water were clear and blue, where mountains and coastlines were perfectly intact, and where architectural wonders are breathtakingly new and unmarred by time and trespasses.

Above the intriguing vista, she can smell the food in the restaurants, hear the chatter in the cafes, move in rhythm to the music in the marketplaces. She materializes on a sophisticated, neatly-arranged city on an uncharted continent, surrounded by the bluest of ocean waters that ebb and flow unto infinity. She can see and feel the exhilaration and vibrancy of the town known as Coronadus where hundreds of men and women build and beautify the landscape with passion and pride.

The streets are laid out symmetrically for easy travel. Every amenity and necessity for a burgeoning civilization is at hand. But it is the great halls that fascinate her: one each for Science and Nature, Medicine and Healing, and Humanistic Understanding.

One more, standing majestically on the highest hill of the landscape, is the Temple of Music and Miracles. It shimmers like a jewel, a monolithic crystalline structure that astonishes the mind with its beauty. That such architecture and ingenuity exist demonstrates a culture with a respect for higher learning and a compassionate social consciousness.

In stark contrast to the architectural beauty is the limestone wall completely surrounding the city, with defensive towers at the main gate that house armed guards. It seems impossible that such a cultured society would ever be the victim of invading armies or entertain the notion of battle, but deep in her psyche she knows it is possible, for a dark side exists in everything and everyone, latent and waiting.

Billie's new life from rebirth to adulthood whizzes by in a blink. Childhood is a blotted-out memory, for it serves no purpose for what she is about to encounter in Coronadus.

She is now known as Mina, a shop girl who works in the Emporium happily serving customers who treat her with courtesy and welcoming smiles. Most of them offer no personal information or ask about her own, but vainly purchase high quality, expensive and often frivolous items, paying cash without asking the price.

Mina's favorite customer is a statuesque woman who hums a lilting melody as she looks over some lovely art pieces, precious items rich in history and beauty that are not just for vanity. Mina has heard rumors the woman is part of a prominent family, is respected and revered, and holds a high position in the community. She wishes this family was her own.

Feeling an immediate and intimate connection to this woman for reasons she has yet to understand, Mina feels free to confide in her.

"I don't really remember my birth family," Mina says. "I don't remember much about anything before I came here. I was told that I was very ill and had amnesia. A kind agency provided passage to Coronadus because they felt the sea air would be healing for me. That's all I know. Otherwise, I usually don't dwell on the past."

"So you are all alone?"

"Yes, I'm afraid so."

"Then please know you have friends here. My family will be yours as well."

Excited about the invitation to have dinner at Bianca's home, Mina wears her favorite pink sheath, actually the only dress she owns that would be appropriate for the dinner.

Elegantly, Bianca wears a colorful caftan and a silk headdress, both with swirls of vivid colors that accentuate blue eyes as clear and deep as the ocean. Mina can only assume that Bianca's hair is flaxen because her complexion is flawlessly ivory.

Her daughter, Saliana, is almost her mother's mirror image, with a cascade of strawberry blonde curls, smooth skin and bright, friendly eyes.

Ishtar on the other hand is a handsome dark-haired man with a neatly trimmed beard to match and a caramel-hued complexion. His and Bianca's niece and nephew, Maati and Sokar, also conform to the native coloring. It was not surprising that Bianca was fair and Ishtar was dark, but that Saliana so favored her mother was curious.

"That was a wonderful meal, Bianca. The best I've had since I moved here."

"Bianca has a culinary mentor who kindly shares her recipes and unique flair for seasonings." This from an unexpected visitor who has just appeared from nowhere.

"Falana," Bianca welcomes her sister. "I didn't expect you so soon. I would have invited you to dinner also, to meet our new friend."

"Thank you, Bianca, I finished at the salon early so I thought I'd pick up my offspring and take them off your hands."

"You know I love having them. Falana, this is Mina, she works at the Emporium and is rather new to Coronadus."

"So nice to meet you, Mina. I'm happy to give you a tour of the city anytime."

"I'd love that, Falana." This girl, with an enviable head of shimmering black waves and pomegranate lips further beautifying a warm complexion, makes Mina even more interested in the diverse bloodline in this family. Silently she laments that her own appearance is an unimpressive, dowdy mop of mouse-brown hair, ruddy complexion and thin, colorless mouth. She feels inadequate in this room of beautiful people.

"In that case I'll come by the Emporium this weekend."

Mina smiles broadly at Falana's decisiveness and confidence, realizing she likes her just as much as she likes Bianca but in a strangely different way.

"Well, I'm pleased you have made a new friend, Mina," Bianca says sincerely.

"So many new friends in one day. I can't thank you enough, Bianca. But I don't want to take advantage of your hospitality any longer, so I will be on my way. Thank you for allowing me to come to your lovely house."

"Oh, please don't go yet. Would you like a tour?"

Everything about the house is expertly crafted, masterfully constructed with clean, uncluttered lines. All the furnishings, the tapestries and drapes, are simple and elegant, neither feminine nor masculine, with splashes of bold color contrasting against white walls. The patio doors are open wide to reveal a beautiful garden of flowers, herbs and vegetables.

"I enjoy the natural life." Bianca says. "I grow many of my season-ings there for cooking, but I never pick the flowers. They belong in their natural home."

It is obvious, as there is not one vase with a colorful spray of blooms on any of the tables. There are no pictures on the tables or breakfront either. Another resistance to the "unnatural" perhaps? But one item captures Mina's attention. On one of the tables near the patio door sits a wooden sculpture, a miniature of a sailing ship in perfect detail, atop a small pedestal to hold it erect.

When Mina admires it, Bianca is evasive. "Oh, just a little something that Ishtar whittled for me," she explains.

"Ishtar," Mina turns to Bianca's husband with a change of subject, "I am intrigued to hear that Saliana is a musician."

"Yes, she is giving a recital at the Temple tomorrow evening. Would you like to attend?"

"Oh, do come," Saliana adds. "It will be fun."

"Yes, yes. I would be honored."

* * *

To arrive at the Temple of Music and Miracles, which sits on the high-est hill of a peninsula, Mina takes the scenic walk across a bridge connecting it to the mainland of Coronadus. Climbing the crystalline steps of the Temple, Mina anticipates something magical is about to happen. Even before she enters the auditorium she feels an energy that enlivens her spirit. Eager people scurry in to find the best seats before the recital begins.

Greeting her in the vestibule, Ishtar and Bianca reassure her. "Don't worry, Mina, we have special VIP seating. It helps to know the star performer - and her music master." Ishtar introduces Mina to Rami, Saliana's mentor.

"Why, I think I know you. I've seen you at the Emporium," Mina says.

"Yes, now and then I appear just to check on my business," Rami tells her.

"You are the proprietor? And yet you have time to teach music?"

"Music is my first love, but as they say, it's good to keep your day occupation."

Mina laments she has no musical talent.

"Everyone has some musical talent," Rami encourages her. "And I'd be happy to help you uncover some of yours. I have a few openings in my teaching schedule if you are interested."

"I don't know what to say. I'd love it but as you know I make a very small salary at the Emporium."

Rami laughs jovially. "Well, let's see. I can give you a raise or some music lessons."

"Oh, music lessons, please."

"As you wish," Rami says. "We will talk after Saliana's performance."

Mina is enthralled with the design of the Temple's auditorium. It is elegant without being ostentatious. The three-tiered theatre holds about 2,000 people in the main floor, the balcony, and in box seats high above the stage where she, Bianca and Ishtar take their places. Although she has no education in sound quality, Mina knows with the first musical note that the acoustics in the room are magnificent.

Saliana is a harpist with a virtuoso's skill and the sensitivity of touch that only a true artist can master. And when she sings, oh when she sings, it is as though an angel has come to visit to give the audience a preview of what heaven sounds like.

Chapter 16

That weekend, with Falana as her personal guide, Mina strolls down every street and climbs high upon vantage points that provide a panoramic view of the city. She is impressed with the landscape, the architecture, and especially the bustling enthusiasm of everyone she encounters. It's as though life isn't moving fast enough and they push it along, cramming all of their personal cravings into each and every day.

"Yes, it can be quite hectic in Coronadus," Falana says, amused by Mina's reaction. "Everyone seems to have something urgent to do or some place important to go. How about something more relaxing, like a boat ride?"

"You have a boat?" Mina's smile is as wide as the sea at the thought of sailing on the clear blue water.

"Yes, we do. My husband Dubri and I go out often. He is quite the sailor. In fact, I have to meet him at the boathouse this afternoon, so come along."

The water ripples and splashes gently at the pilings of the boathouse. Mina and Falana approach one of the vessels, a sleek cutter with an additional sail between the headsail and the mainsail, all of which are still wrapped up and tied down. Still, one can see the vibrant colors of the silk and canvas cloth, which Mina surmises is breathtaking when they unfurl.

They walk up the gangway to the deck and notice that the door of the boathouse is wide open waiting for boats that are ready to cruise out of the channel into the open water.

While Falana moves aft to check the life jackets and other paraphernalia, Mina walks around deck running her hands along the smooth polished rails and taking in the mystical experience of being aboard such a lovely craft. Voices capture her attention and she walks toward them, but they come from below and carry through the small doors of the lower cabin, which are slightly ajar. She tries not to eavesdrop but what she hears confuses her.

From what she can gather, Mina overhears Dubri and his friend Sechmet talking about an "operation" - a plan to collude with some comrades from a distant land who want to help take over Coronadus. They believe there to be some valuable and powerful crystals buried here that can conjure a legendary great ship that contains all the knowledge of the universe. It is suspected that Bianca's family has possession and Bianca knows where they are.

Hearing the men start up the stairs, Mina scurries to Falana's side trying to make small talk.

"It's a beautiful boat, Falana. Can you tell me about it? Does it have a motor as well as sails?"

"Yes. It has sails and engines both. The engines propel the boats out of calm areas and into the path of predicted winds where the sails are hoisted. The engines are then cut so we can cruise along and enjoy the silence."

"But not just any kind of engine," Dubri now interjects. "They have special transmitters and can be operated from the shore, just in case our equipment fails. Then we are not just adrift with no way home."

"Really? That's amazing. Remote-controlled sailboats. I don't think I've ever heard of that. But then I know nothing at all about sailboats."

"Dubri, where did Sechmet go?" Falana asks, not seeing her husband's friend. "Wasn't he down in the cabin with you?"

"He's gone," Dubri answers firmly without explanation. "Let's get going and take our guest on a beautiful voyage."

Deftly, Dubri unties the sails one by one and lets them fly, controlling each one masterfully so the wind fills them from behind.

In such an idyllic setting, Mina closes her eyes as the chilly breeze and salt water caress her face and the bright sun soothes her cares. She momentarily forgets the foreboding she felt hearing Dubri and Sechmet plot against her friend Bianca.

But later, she recounts the conversation.

"Falana is a friend, too, Bianca. And what I heard concerns me, for both of you. What's going on? Can I help in any way?"

"Thank you, Mina. You were right to tell me. I've suspected for a long time that Dubri has sinister tendencies. Before she met Dubri, Falana and I were very close. Our family was highly respected on Coronadus, and very much trusted. That was the legacy my father gave to us, one of integrity and honesty. I was fortunate to have married Ishtar, a brilliant and compassionate man and a visionary designer.

"Falana was not so fortunate. She met Dubri, the ultimate charmer who could wrap Falana around his finger. After she married him, we discovered he is a miscreant," Bianca speaks the word with contempt, "involved in one shady deal after another until he lost our respect. I warned Falana to get away from him, but she seems both intoxicated and fearful at the same time."

"He is very forceful," Mina agrees. "Every time he demanded something on our sailing, Falana jumped but she tried to keep a positive attitude, smiling at me and shrugging off his gruffness. But what's this about crystals he speaks of? So powerful they can conjure up some great mystery ship that they want to get their hands on? And why would he collude with Sechmet to allow enemies of Coronadus to come here, bringing danger with them?"

"I can't go into detail about this, Mina. If they knew you had any information your life would be in jeopardy. Suffice it to say that my family, particularly my father, may he rest in peace, had possession of these powerful crystals and secured them away in a place where no one could find them except, at some point in the future, their rightful owner - someone who would use their power for good and righteous purposes."

"And the ship?"

"A vessel that can only be invoked by that same person who gains possession of the crystals and knows how to use them."

Mina glances at the small wooden sculpture of a ship that sits on the table. "Does it have to do with that? Is Ishtar the rightful owner? Does he know where the crystals are?"

Bianca is careful with her words. "Let's just say that Ishtar has a wonderful imagination and whittled that boat as a reminder for me of what my father and his wise friends stood for. No, Ishtar is not the rightful owner of the crystals, nor am I. And neither of us knows where they are. But that doesn't stop Dubri and Sechmet from being suspicious of me."

"What you have told me will be kept secret forever, Bianca. "I will do whatever you want me to do."

* * *

Under the cover of night a group of swarthy militants disembark their boat and meet Dubri and Sechmet in a secluded cove out of sight of the guard towers.

"We have a cache of weapons on board that will overpower anyone who tries to stop us."

"Don't worry," Dubri tells them, "we will take them completely by surprise. The City Council is meeting in the Justice Hall tonight. There are no weapons there. We will knock off a few of them to let them know we mean business and take one or two hostages for leverage. Here is a map, but stay put until I radio you to proceed."

When Sechmet and Dubri get to the Civic Center they find the Hall of Justice is empty. They are angry and Sechmet takes it out on his accomplice.

"What is this, Dubri? You don't even have your intelligence right."

Exasperated, Dubri declares, "They always meet mid-week. They have never missed a session in 10 years."

Sechmet sees a janitor who tells them that the Hall is undergoing maintenance for an electrical outage. They had to move the meeting at the last minute.

"Did they say where they were going?"

"No. I thought they just canceled it. Everyone was told to go home."

Sechmet doesn't buy it but doesn't want to rouse the janitor's suspicions. He radios the crew to hold off. He needs to find out where Bianca and the council went.

Mina and Falana encounter Dubri and Sechmet on the square. "Who is at home with Maati and Sokar?"

"Don't worry," Dubri assures his wife. "I have the neighbors watching them for awhile. But I thought they were going to be with your sister tonight."

"No, she has a meeting with the Council, I believe."

"Oh, that explains it," Dubri says. "Good. I have some business to bring to them."

"If it's the one in the Justice Hall, I think it's been canceled," Mina says. "I overheard some people talking."

"That's strange," Falana says. "I saw her heading toward the Civic Center earlier."

"I need you to find out for me, Falana. I have some urgent business to take up with them so I need to know where they are meeting and when."

"What makes you think I know?"

"She's your sister. Find out," Dubri demands.

"Oh, for heaven's sake, Dubri. Do you have to be so rude?"

"Let's talk about this somewhere else. Dubri takes his wife's elbow and pushes her along.

Feeling uncomfortable and wishing she hadn't even said a word about the canceled meeting, Mina takes her leave. "I think I'd better get on home now, Falana. Thank you for a nice visit. We'll do it again."

"Oh - yes, Mina. We will. I'm sorry to have to leave you so abruptly."

Dubri and Falana walk in the opposite direction as Mina who turns and makes her way toward home. But a voice in her head forewarns her to secretly follow them and find out what Dubri is up to.

At the cove, Sechmet and the insurgents work on an ambush strategy to execute once they discover the location of the Council meeting. One man, however, feels this is insufficient. "Once we overtake the Council and secure a hostage, we will need a more far-reaching plan to infiltrate the city and tyrannize the citizens. We can't give them time or incentive to fight back."

"What do you have in mind?" Sechmet asks.

"Who or what do they value or revere most? If we can discover that and either capture it or destroy it, they'll be cowed into submission."

"I know exactly *who* they revere most and *what* she values above all else," Sechmet asserts. "She will be our target. Okay, this is what we will do first..."

Chapter 17

Dubri answers a call from Sechmet stating that one of his informants discovered the Council secretly meeting in the Coronadus church.

"The church? How many are there?" He is evasive for Falana's sake. "I mean, are there many items on the agenda and other citizens there to make a presentation?"

"Just the Council members and Bianca."

"Good. Uh - thank you for the information. I will go and make my case."

"Well, it seems they are meeting at the church this evening. I need you to come with me, Falana, and help me convince Bianca to let me speak my piece to the Council."

"What about the children? It will be very late by the time we get home?"

"The neighbor will agree to keep them a few hours more, so don't worry."

"What is so important that you have to inconvenience me and our neighbor like this?"

"It's my chance, Falana, - *our* chance - to be wealthy and powerful, by taking control of Coronadus. Bianca is weak, she and her artsy family. They don't know what strength is. The city is dying with their high-minded approach to every issue."

"Bianca is not weak. She heads the council and she's the one you have to convince. You know how headstrong she can be. What will you do, Dubri?"

"Nothing terrible, Falana. I will always protect you and our children. But if Bianca and the Council won't change their ways willingly we will have to stage a coup."

"Who is this *we* you speak of? What kind of coup?"

"Friends from a neighboring island. They have a fail-proof plan that worked for them. We just have to convince the citizens of Coronadus that it's a better way."

Thankful that Falana loves fresh air and has left a window open in her house, Mina is able to overhear the entire conversation. She makes a heart-pounding run to the church to inform Bianca.

"Knowing Sechmet and Dubri they will try and use force," Bianca says. "So we must be prepared with a defensive plan."

A small cadre of Coronadus security guards are on alert and stationed on the church roof with a 360-degree view of the city, believing that insurgents will have no cover no matter which direction they come from.

As the council convenes, Falana enters and addresses the members but primarily her sister.

"Please listen to what my husband has to say. His ideas are bold and innovative. I think that's what we need to help move Coronadus forward into a new age."

"Your words or his, dear sister?"

"Both," Dubri states, coming forward assertively. "Falana supports me as always. But I need your support as well, Bianca."

"And just what is it you propose?" a Councilwoman interjects with others adding their own concerns including Bianca who casts a wary eye.

"We need to restructure the governing body - including the Council. I want to throw my hat in the ring as the Chairman and have voting privileges."

"You know that we have a procedure for that, a very democratic one. We can't just dub you the leader in a closed-door session."

"Under ordinary circumstances I would agree. But we don't have time to fool around with elections and campaigns and ballot resolutions. That's for fools who still believe democracy works."

"What you're proposing is a dictatorship, Dubri. And we will have none of it." Bianca is unequivocal.

"Really? So you've made that decision unilaterally without hearing me out and taking a vote? Who's the dictator now?"

"So speak your piece," a member tells him, impatient.

"I propose a coalition government, with experts from other nations to come and be part of it. I am well prepared to execute such a plan."

"You have done nothing to contribute to the growth of Coronadus to be making such bold propositions," Bianca admonishes. "You've cheated your neighbors and your clients and found surreptitious ways to skirt prosecution." She addresses the Council directly. "The list is long and sordid, as everyone on the Council knows."

"And what has Bianca done to hold such a position of esteem? She was not elected? She was anointed to it!"

"It is her birthright , Dubri. She inherited it through her parents and their parents before."

"The Chosen One." Dubri scoffs.

"And then she allowed the democratic process to be cultivated and implemented in an orderly and fair manner."

"And what has it gotten you? Oh, yes, you have your magnificent halls, temples and educational institutions, beautiful landscapes and architecture, but if enemies were to burst through the gates you could not defend the city. Your weapons are sorely out of date and no match for the munitions that every other surrounding nation has developed."

"Are you proposing war, Dubri?" Bianca probes further. "Or are you threatening us with one?"

"I am just warning you that there are people in this town who are tired of the status quo and want change, especially economic and political change."

"Our people have everything they could want in Coronadus, Dubri. Don't think you can so easily take that away from us."

"We shall see, Bianca." Dubri leaves in a huff and radios the crew to execute their plan. "They will be easy to overtake," he tells them.

"Please, Bianca. Don't dismiss him out of hand," Falana beseeches. "Please heed what Dubri is saying. Change needs to come to Coronadus if we are to prosper and compete in the world."

"Falana, you know more than what you are telling me. What is Dubri really up to? What will he do now?"

"I don't know for sure, Bianca. I only know I love you just as much as I love my husband and don't want to see anything happen to either of you."

"Your vague references tell me all I need to know, that I am right to be wary of your husband and his motives."

"You never did like him, never supported my marriage to him," Falana pouts. "I'm trying to help and all you do is cast aspersions."

"Do the right thing, Falana," Bianca admonishes her sister. "You know what the right thing is. I don't have to tell you."

Angry and confused, Falana runs from the church smack into Mina, who tries to stop her. Falana is angry at her sister but she will try to keep Dubri from doing anything violent. "He is my husband and I have no choice but to help him."

"What do you mean you have no choice. Did he threaten you?"

"Not really. But I know he would try to turn my children against me if I didn't go along. I don't want to be my sister's adversary. But she is so stubborn and belittling."

"She loves you, Falana. She would protect you. Please let her."

"As I said. I have no choice."

Torn between them, Mina cannot choose which friend to be loyal to so she tries to protect them both.

"Let me go with you, Falana," Mina offers. "Maybe I can help sway Dubri to wait and be patient, to give Bianca time to consult with the Council before he takes some action that he can't undo."

"No, Mina. Dubri doesn't know you. He would never listen. He is quite chauvinistic. Please be careful and stay out of the fray, Mina. I wouldn't forgive myself if anything happened to you."

With that, Falana turns heel and hurries home.

Chapter 18

The confrontation is a violent one. The gang of interlopers, hiding discreetly amongst the ordinary citizenry, move in undetected by the church guards. Stealthily they climb the wall ladders and, attacking from behind, pick them off like sitting ducks, rendering each one impotent or dead. Swiftly they rush the church and overtake the entire Council. Bianca is their target and the secret cache of sacred crystals is the treasure they hunt.

"I will never tell you anything," Bianca vows. "No matter what you do to me."

"Not even if we kill every member of your precious Council?"

"Don't give in, Bianca." They all stand united behind her. "Better to die than to live under tyranny."

"No one will die while I have a breath in my body," Bianca declares.

"Please, Bianca! Give them what they want. I can't lose you!" Falana enters, armed against her will, but willing to do anything to save her sister.

"Falana! Go!" Bianca orders her. "You have children who need you. I will be protected."

"Yes, she will!" It is Mina now who moves between Falana and Bianca. "Please, Falana, you are my friend, too. I would hate to have anything happen to either of you."

One of the insurgents grabs Bianca to hold her hostage, then orders every member of the Council out of the building. "If you know what is good for all of you, or for your precious Bianca, you will leave and tell no one what is happening here tonight."

"No!" Dubri now demands. "They will not leave here alive. Citizens will be swarming around the church in no time. Kill them all!"

"No, Dubri!" Falana protests.

In a merciless hail of gunfire, every member of the Council is cut down where they stand, blood spewing everywhere defacing the sanctity of the holy place.

Mina runs to Falana and tries to protect her. Dubri aims his revolver at Mina but hits Falana instead. She is stunned motionless for a second, her eyes questioning, then drops to the floor.

"Falana! Falana!" Mina screams. "Dubri, what have you done?"

Bianca breaks free from the tyrant holding her and rushes toward her sister. Dubri aims his gun at Bianca but Mina pushes his hand up and they struggle for the weapon. It falls to the floor out of Dubri's reach.

Suddenly, from behind, Mina is stabbed violently.

Bianca throws herself at Dubri's gun, grabs it, aims expertly and kills Mina's assailant with one bullet. Dubri and the murdering gang scatter from the church to find Sechmet and plan their next move. In the end, all but one member of the council lies brutally murdered. Bianca.

Heartbroken at the sight of her sister's lifeless body, Bianca covers her face with her hands, drained and shaken by the violence. She shakes her head as though to make the image disappear and cries out, "Falana was just a child. What did she know about such things? How did she make such a bad decision? What could I have done to stop her?"

"Nothing, Bianca..." Mina is speaking now, forcing the words from her mouth as she feels life leaving her body. "We make... our own decisions... good or bad..." As her eyesight fades, the image of her sister, Fallon, looms large, morphing gently into Falana's spirit. Together, as one, their tragic journeys over at last, Fallon and Falana become sister souls, comforting one another, dissolving into their intended bliss.

Rushing to her friend's side, Bianca kneels down, cradles her head and strokes her face." And you, Mina - you hardly knew me yet you sacrificed your life for me." Bianca sobs, now holding Mina in her arms.

Breathing shallowly, gasping for air, Mina apologizes for not being able to help.

"You have nothing to be sorry for, dearest. Nothing."

"There is... one thing I ...do regret..."

"What is that, my dear friend?"

Mina smiles at the irony of her final thought. "I'll never have Rami...teach me music... I so wanted to learn..."

"You will have music wherever you are, Mina. Glorious, divine, heavenly music." Bianca rocks Mina gently, humming to her sweetly so that her voice is the last sound Mina will hear. In death as in life they are kindred souls with the same mission - to protect the people they love. And they both failed.

But in a joyful, final rush of ecstasy Mina imagines her aura unifying with Bianca's. The transformation is translucent at first, shimmering and ephemeral. Now it takes shape, form, content, a vision so warm, so embracing that Mina moves toward it, willingly, longingly, unafraid. Her gold hair moves freely, the pink sheath caresses her spirit body gently. She is vibrant, breathtaking, alive. She is Mina, then Bianca, then Billie Nickerson again, and a familiar voice calls to her, *"Take the journey, Billie. Take the journey and I will take it with you."*

* * *

Resentment and pain form a heavy veil across Bianca's face, but she steels herself to go on. Funerals and memorials fill the days and nights of Coronadus. Heavy hearts, guilt and anguish are not easily assuaged, for they know that their lives and their hometown have been irreparably altered.

Small bands of thugs stage raids almost nightly looking for the sacred crystals that will give them the power to conjure the Moon Singer, the ship of legend that holds all the wisdom and knowledge of the universe in her masts. The small bands turn into marching armies who confiscate every weapon and every means of resistance, rendering the townspeople impotent; but, to a one they promise to protect Bianca and her family.

Vowing to defeat them, Bianca implores Ishtar to take Saliana away, to keep her safe in the Temple of Music and Miracles and destroy the bridge that connects it to the mainland.

"I will stay behind, "Bianca vows, "to join the underground to help save our people. You must protect Saliana's gift, her music, from those who would use it for their own benefit. And especially protect the Rose Crystal."

"I can't leave you here to their mercy," Ishtar protests. "Please come with us."

"You know, I can't. I have an obligation to fulfill. We always knew one day I would have to defend my legacy."

"Please be careful, Bianca. You know there is only one recourse to end this siege. It could destroy everything we know and hold dear."

"Or it can save it."

Reluctantly, Ishtar and Saliana agree to go. They bid farewell to their beloved Bianca and agree to come back when the war has been won.

But in a surprise attack on the town square, when bombs and incendiaries destroy the church and the schoolhouse, many Coronadans die, including Sechmet's little girl, Marena. Inconsolable, he vows revenge on "The Chosen One," but Bianca tries to make peace with Sechmet, knowing both have lost loved ones to this horrible battle that should never have been waged.

"None of this would ever have happened if you hadn't been so obstinate and let us know where the crystals are."

"I've told you, I don't know where they are. That was how my father protected me, to keep me ignorant of their whereabouts."

"Someone is bound to find them one day, Bianca. You know it to be true."

"But not me, or you, or those thugs you have aligned yourself with to turn against your own people."

Still believing that Bianca is lying, Sechmet feigns submission and reluctantly urges the invaders to leave when their search for the coveted crystals bears no fruit. "Leave it be for now," Sechmet negotiates. "I will call upon you again one day, when all has quieted down. I will befriend Bianca and when I have gained her confidence I will get her to reveal where we can find the treasure."

"We can't trust that you will share this information with us, Sechmet. We are not leaving. We will be watching Bianca and watching you."

* * *

It is her shame and her guilt. To have survived at the expense of someone else's life still haunts her. More than once she should have died, but some unexplained force intervened and saved Bianca's life. This time it was Mina who was a conduit for that power. She wishes she had died along with them, with Falana and Mina. Better yet, saved them. Yet, she knows that being spared, to be "The Chosen One," has only one purpose: to protect the crystals and the great ship Moon Singer to be discovered by their one true owner.

Seeing the despair of her fellow citizens, knowing that the danger for them still lingers because of the existence of the sacred gems that others would kill for, Bianca determines that there is only one solution.

"The old must be destroyed so the new can be resurrected," Bianca declares. "The heritage of my ancestors will be safe and saved for the next soul who will find, cherish, and use the knowledge for good."

Taking the small sculpture of the Moon Singer, the wooden likeness of the great ship that Ishtar whittled, into her hands, fully cognizant of the wisdom it holds, Bianca meditates on her next action. Through the night and until the sun breaks through in a glorious burst of dawn, Bianca allows the essence of the tiny ship to enlighten her. The choice is now clear. Her fateful decision is made.

Opening a drawer in her private desk, Bianca lifts the ancient artifact from its locked box. The beauty of the spherical piece with eight points spread equally around to resemble the petals of a flower, with the final point in the shape of a golden *fleur de lis*, never ceases to fill Bianca's soul with an awesome reverence. It is the instrument that has guided travelers and mariners to their destinations for centuries, and now allows Bianca to use its celestial power to shape the destiny of Coronadus and all its inhabitants.

It is time to use The Wind Rose.

Chapter 19

Welcoming Billie back to her place in the Afterlife, the Elders explain how the people she encountered in her many unique incarnations are like family, and why she herself has been both student and teacher.

"We all exist in an endless cycle of life and death, our souls intertwining through many lifetimes. We meet as parent and child, as husband and wife, as lover and friend, and as mother and son. Our roles are interchanged constantly so that we may experience the highs and lows of emotion, the riches and poverty of the social hierarchy, the violence and peace of the world order, and the pain and passion of life so that we gain empathy. We learn and teach what we have learned, only to realize we still have more to learn and to teach."

"I understand that now," Billie concedes. "I am at once exhausted and exhilarated by the experiences. But, I am beginning to know what my Nameless guide calls the cloud of amnesia, forgetting my previous lives and letting go of my attachment to them. Yet, there is one yearning that still haunts my memory, and I cannot seem to release it. Nor do I want to."

"It is not within our purview to clarify that for you," the Elders tell her. "However, because of your selfless act of saving another's life at the expense of your own, you have earned the privilege of making your case to the Other - the only one who can permit you to return to earth one more time to discover what that one true desire is."

"Yes, Billie Nickerson," the Other addresses her, "I have known of your longing ever since you entered our realm. Devoted and caring spirit guides have intervened on your behalf more than once, but knew you were not ready for such a transformation. It seems that you are now. You are ready to recognize and fulfill your personal mission. However, it will not be as simple or clear as you might prefer."

Billie sighs deeply, not wanting to ask. "You don't mean more irrelevant life experiences, more earthly meanderings? No clear purpose or karmic finality?"

"There are no irrelevant life experiences," the Other explains. "They are all threads in a tapestry that form a pattern revealing your destiny."

"I don't understand. I don't see a pattern yet. Just fragments of a whole thing that don't mesh."

"Do you recall what dreams are like? Remnants of happenings that seem realistic while you sleep but make no sense when you wake up?"

"I've had many of those abstract, indecipherable dreams," Billie admits. "Was I too inept to understand their meanings?"

"Yes. And no," the Other replies vaguely.

"Stop! Stop! This is all so cryptic. Puzzles that don't fit, tapestries without a pattern, dreams that are elusive. Why *me?* What is the purpose of all of this intrigue? When will I know what I am to do?"

"You know what you are to do. Your mission is a heroic one and much is asked of you, perhaps more than most souls. Just keep your focus. You know what to do."

A bleakness of spirit washes over her tinged with exasperation for all she has endured. She dares to ask:

"They call you Other, but are you - are you *God?*"

"What do you think?"

"I - I don't know. I think if you were God you would not even be visible to me. Your image would be so brilliant I could not look at you without shielding my eyes. At least, so the legend goes."

"The legend?"

"You know. The story. I'm not a religious person. But it's something that people who have religious experiences often describe."

"And what do you see?" the Other asks.

"I'm not sure. I see your essence and it is strong and warm and comforting. It is nothing I have ever seen before but it also feels like looking into a mirror," Billie replies.

"And so, what do you think?"

"I think - whoever or whatever you are, I need your wisdom, your guidance, the power that you have to grant my wish."

"The power and wisdom is within you, Billie Nickerson. What you want is yours to manifest."

"I haven't done a good job of it so far. I couldn't save my parents from being murdered, or save my sister from being shot. I couldn't save myself from dying too soon! And so now I meander from life to life."

"Billie, don't you realize that each incarnation is an opportunity for redemption? In your last life you displayed selfless courage, and it has brought you to this point."

"Yes. To this point. There is something I must do but I am forgetting. The purpose is slipping away."

The Other pauses briefly, contemplating a decision that will change the course of Billie's destiny forever.

"Because your task is so important," the Other states, "and your journey is a long and arduous one, I will help you to remember."

The clarity of what she must do is beginning to fade but the passion for it, the urgency of it, remains. Billie ponders for a moment, knowing this is her last chance, hoping that what she chooses is the right and righteous decision.

Grateful that she will have help in remembering, she entreats:

"And how shall I come to Earth this time, in what form and which incarnation? Do I have the will to try again?"

Other: Of course, here there is no "will" – there is only doing, being, and knowing.

"But I have so grown tired of the journeys, the repetitive teaching of the same lesson over and over again, only to be disappointed by resistance."

Other: Then teach a new lesson, or the same Truth, in a new way. Until it is imbued into bodies, minds and hearts, and then believed, you will continue to make the sojourns.

"A multitude of times, I have made my presence felt but not known, not revealing who or what I am. Isn't it time to do so? Reveal, that is?"

Other: It depends on your subject. Would he or she be ready to accept this knowledge?

"There could be danger there, if the knowledge is used unwisely, or with self-serving motives. My...the subject... best for receiving would be someone who has a grand purpose beyond his or her own fulfillment."

Other: An innocent, perhaps. Someone who has never thought to seek such knowledge - yet.

"But where will this One be found?"

Other: In the past and present, in the heavens and on earth, in time and space. And in his mother's heart.

"Mother's heart?"

Other: In recognizing her heart's desire, you will find this One that you seek, whose own purpose you will recognize immediately.

"And that is...?"

Other: To save a life that means more to him than his own.

"But how shall I reveal myself to him?"

Other: Uniquely. In a most extraordinary and magnificent way.

Epilogue - One Final Journey

So Billie will be with the ones she loves as someone they recognize in their hearts but do not know. She will be there as they go through their lives in reality and in dreams, in the past, present and future, in fantasies and wishes. She will be there to walk by their side, to guide them to their higher purpose, through sadness and confusion to their happiness and serenity.

She will be there for David in the flutter of a breeze, in the music in his heart, in his anger and in his forgiveness. When he feels he has nowhere to turn, when much is asked of him that he cannot comprehend, when heroic deeds are required that are beyond the scope of his experiences or abilities, she will be there.

When he is inspired to magical ideas and believes in miracles that no mortal can manifest, with each new adventure, with every success and failure, in his confusion and in his revelations, she will be there.

When he can hold in the palm of his hand the vehicle that allows him to transcend time and space and journey to world's beyond, and then find his way home again...

When he hears what others cannot and ultimately hears and recognizes his soul's song...

She will be there.

* * *

And so, Dorinda's plan unfolds.

The End

The story continues in
The Moon Singer Trilogy

Book One: *The Crystal Clipper*

"*The Crystal Clipper*" is the fairy tale adventure, for this is how we all begin to deal with life - by daydreaming fantastic ways to deal with life's problems. For David, the princess imprisoned in the tower, the monsters, the deceptions and Temptations in the Prism Palace represent the conflicts and fears of everyday life.

David Nickerson begins his fantastic journeys as a boy trying to cope with a series of family crises: his Father's unemployment, his sister's paralysis, the death of his mother, and his deafness after a serious illness.

When David acquires a sacred *Singer* crystal, he conjures up the supernaturally-powered clipper ship *Moon Singer,* which takes him on spectacular sojourns to past and future lifetimes. The people he encounters all have a soul connection to one another and their lives are destined to intertwine many times over.

With the help of a young princess who has the power of healing in her song, David is ultimately transformed into a young man who can "hear" what others cannot and who can "see" what others deny. But his mission is always the same - to save a life that means more to him than his own.

Book Two: *The War Chamber*

"*The War Chamber*" is David's trial by fire. This unwitting hero, who became captain of the mystical sailing ship *Moon Singer* and saved his sister's life on a mythical Island of Darkness, has yet to learn that his deafness is his greatest gift. It is this "disability," and his possession of three sacred artifacts: The Singer Crystal, The Rose Crystal, and now The Wind Rose Compass, that allow David the power to save the lives of everyone he loves.

While David's Nickerson's home town fights passionately over how to revive a stagnant economy, he is despondent that all the miracles he brought back with him on the Moon Singer have dissipated. He is just as deaf as before, his sister's paralysis has returned, and his anguish over his mother's death is stronger than ever.

David goes to her gravesite, determined to try and communicate with her through his crystals, and understand why she left him all alone to grieve for her. Instead, he finds himself transported to a strange city of fascinating people who are caught in a time warp between a high-tech, materialistic and militant past and their penchant for a simpler, more peaceful way of life.

It is here that David encounters a revered woman who becomes like a mother to him and helps him understand how his deafness and his mother's karmic mission are intertwined. When a cataclysmic event destroys the city, David learns that the past, present and future know no boundaries, that they are one in the unending circle of life.

Returning to his home town's remarkable transformation, David realizes that he must face up to his obligations as captain of the *Moon Singer* and follow his destiny, wherever it may lead.

Book Three: *The Wind Rose*

In this third and final adventure, the prophecy of the Moon Singer is realized. But it all revolves around the answer to one question: Can music actually create and destroy life?

If David, whose deafness still eludes treatment, cannot hear it, will he be able to tap into music's power to save the planet from catastrophe? Only if he is able to reunite the three sacred artifacts: the Singer crystal, the Rose Crystal pendant, and the Wind Rose compass. Their Triune energy is all that David needs to re-harmonize the destructive discordant music created by a vengeful music master.

The mystical clipper ship *Moon Singer* is David's transport to the Source of his paranormal abilities, but only through his complete understanding of the Power of Three to Become One will he manifest his destiny and once again save a life that means more to him than his own. That understanding will come to him when he deciphers the cryptic musical codes that have been created for evil purposes.

In unraveling these codes David will come to know his own soul's song, the one that allows his disability to become his greatest gift.

Dear reader,

We hope you enjoyed reading *Before The Boy*. Please take a moment to leave a review, even if it's a short one. Your opinion is important to us.

Discover more books by B. Roman at
https://www.nextchapter.pub/authors/b-roman

Want to know when one of our books is free or discounted? Join the newsletter at http://eepurl.com/bqqB3H

Best regards,
B. Roman and the Next Chapter Team

The story continues in:

The Crystal Clipper by B. Roman

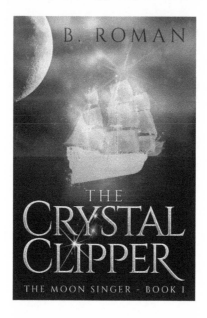

To read the first chapter for free, please head to:
https://www.nextchapter.pub/books/the-crystal-clipper

Before The Boy
ISBN: 978-4-86750-806-0

Published by
Next Chapter
1-60-20 Minami-Otsuka
170-0005 Toshima-Ku, Tokyo
+818035793528
15th June 2021